Dial Emmy for Murder

"A fast-paced, fun-reading novel. Soap opera fans will take pleasure in the behind-the-scenes look from the perspective of someone deeply embedded in the industry; those who don't follow the daytime shows will still enjoy the entertaining characters and the delightful, if undemanding, murder-mystery plot. The engaging interplay between Alexis and Jakes is an added bonus. This is a winning series that makes for a perfect companion to the beach this summer."
—Mysterious Reviews

"Talk about art imitating life. . . . [Davidson] brings her soap experiences into this chilling whodunit. Soap fans will know the author uses anecdotes from each show she performed on . . . an entertaining tale."
—Genre Go Round Reviews

"An enjoyable, lighthearted murder mystery with a solid story and very likable characters. Go pick up your copy today and read, read, read!"
—The Long and the Short of It

"An enjoyable mystery with plenty of insider info that fans of daytime dramas will eat up."
—The Mystery Reader

"[Davidson's] experiences in the field have helped color her books and make them fun and realistic . . . [a] fun read from page one."   —Armchair Interviews

continued . . .

"Eileen Davidson's behind-the-scenes peeks into the world of daytime television are great fun, and *Dial Emmy for Murder*'s crimes, car chases, and mystery adventures are exciting without being gruesome. Even the romance is fun but safe for sensitive readers, which is just the way I like it."　　　—Blue Ribbon Reviews

Death in Daytime

"A fun read. Eileen's many years as a daytime television star add verisimilitude to her novel's soap opera backdrop, as her heroine struggles to clear her name while finding romance in this fast-paced whodunit. A little guilty pleasure for soap opera fans and nonfans alike."
　　　　　—Kay Alden, former head writer of *The Young and the Restless* and associate head writer of *The Bold and the Beautiful*

"Through the character of Alexis, we get a real inside perspective on the life of a soap opera veteran—not a clichéd diva, but a warm, complex, and thoughtful single mother with a great sense of humor about herself and the 'glamorous' world she works in. . . . Readers will be thrilled with the unexpected twists and turns of the plot. I know I was."
　　　　　—Peter Bergman (Jack Abbott on *The Young and the Restless*)

"Eileen Davidson's debut mystery has star quality with an appealing protagonist and fascinating lore about the making of TV soaps."
　　　　　—*New York Times* bestselling author Carolyn Hart

"[A] funny and entertaining read that had me laughing out loud. Ms. Davidson draws on a world she knows very well and gives you a host of 'who did it' characters that keeps you guessing to the very end. I highly recommend this book and can see it as a movie."
　　　　　—Ronn Moss (Ridge Forrester on *The Bold and the Beautiful*)

"The author clearly knows her milieu and brings her characters and setting to life. There are a lot of natural suspects together with a good amount of misdirection, the result being a credible whodunit."

—Mysterious Reviews

"Readers get treated to the inside scoop of what happens at a popular soap opera offscreen as Eileen Davidson uses her experience on *The Young and the Restless* and *The Bold and the Beautiful* to create the background to this exciting, heady, and enthralling mystery. . . . With great characters, a fun look at soaping, and an engaging whodunit, fans beyond the soaps will enjoy this fine amateur sleuth tale."

—Genre Go Round Reviews

"Ms. Davidson is an actress, and clearly knows the inner workings of daytime dramas. She's great at giving the reader an inside look at the real-life soap behind the soap. . . . You'll find this to be a fast, frothy read. The author's breezy writing style really makes the whole caper fun, without going over the top."

—CA Reviews

"In this fast-paced and entertaining mystery that takes place on the set of a soap opera, *The Young and the Restless* star Davidson's heroine has an engaging voice laced with humor and irony. . . . This glimpse into the daytime television world is interesting and informative, and one need not be a soap fan to enjoy the well-plotted, suspenseful story." —*Romantic Times*

Also by Eileen Davidson

Death in Daytime
Dial Emmy for Murder

Eileen Davidson

Diva
Las Vegas

A SOAP OPERA MYSTERY

AN OBSIDIAN MYSTERY

OBSIDIAN

Published by New American Library, a division of
Penguin Group (USA) Inc., 375 Hudson Street,
New York, New York 10014, USA
Penguin Group (Canada), 90 Eglinton Avenue East, Suite 700, Toronto,
Ontario M4P 2Y3, Canada (a division of Pearson Penguin Canada Inc.)
Penguin Books Ltd., 80 Strand, London WC2R 0RL, England
Penguin Ireland, 25 St. Stephen's Green, Dublin 2,
Ireland (a division of Penguin Books Ltd.)
Penguin Group (Australia), 250 Camberwell Road, Camberwell, Victoria 3124,
Australia (a division of Pearson Australia Group Pty. Ltd.)
Penguin Books India Pvt. Ltd., 11 Community Centre, Panchsheel Park,
New Delhi - 110 017, India
Penguin Group (NZ), 67 Apollo Drive, Rosedale, North Shore 0632,
New Zealand (a division of Pearson New Zealand Ltd.)
Penguin Books (South Africa) (Pty.) Ltd., 24 Sturdee Avenue,
Rosebank, Johannesburg 2196, South Africa

Penguin Books Ltd., Registered Offices:
80 Strand, London WC2R 0RL, England

First published by Obsidian, an imprint of New American Library,
a division of Penguin Group (USA) Inc.

First Printing, July 2010
10 9 8 7 6 5 4 3 2 1

ACKNOWLEDGMENTS

Thanks to Marthayn Pelegrimas for her invaluable work on this manuscript.

Chapter 1

"Honey, that girl is butt naked!"

"No, she's not."

"Alex! She's naked and so is the girl next to her. Look right there." He pointed to an area below her waist.

I took a step closer, looking in the general direction his finger was pointing, and tried to be as discreet as possible.

"Ew!" I said, turning away. "You're right! She is naked." I couldn't believe what I was seeing, so I looked again, just to make sure. At first glance, the girl appeared to be wearing a tuxedo, complete with black tie and tails. The girl next to her looked like a mermaid. Sparkles and scales everywhere. And I do mean everywhere. But it was paint. Meticulously applied and not a detail missed on either of them.

As I took another peek, I winced.

"How did they get the paint right there? Awkward."

Talk about an assault to the senses. We had just stepped out of the limo and into the most flamboyant, intense party in the world—we were at the infamous Playboy Mansion. I hadn't been there since I was in my early twenties.

The main house was a "traditional" Tudor-style mansion. But that night was the Annual Halloween Bash. Tombstones lay scattered across the sprawling lawn, and bodies squirmed to free themselves from their graves. There were cobwebs hanging from windows and doors. Giant ghouls and ghosts (people on stilts) walked the grounds, chasing half-naked women into the darkness. The party had started at eight p.m. It was ten thirty now, and it looked to be in full swing.

In front of the mansion, by the driveway, was a large haunted house Hugh Hefner set up every year. A line of about forty people waited to get in, and from what I had heard, it was well worth the wait. It had taken a week to put together, and everyone I had talked to said it was the most frightening haunted house they'd ever experienced. I was trying to take it all in when I heard my name.

"Hey, Alex! Nice outfit!" she said sarcastically.

"Hi, Shana. I know, I know. I ordered it online. Not exactly like the picture."

I knew I had to get sexy for Hef's party, so I chose a Little Bo Peep outfit. It seemed like a good idea at the time. How was I supposed to know there'd be so many ruffles? I didn't feel particularly sexy with a pile of blond ringlets on my head and a big blue bow on my butt, not to mention petticoats jutting out and knocking over everything in my path. I was carrying a staff to finish off the look. George thought it would be funny if he went as a sheep. Get it? Little Bo Peep has lost her sheep? I wasn't thrilled with the idea, but George had really pushed for it. He's my best friend and hairdresser—and brilliant at both.

George is only five feet four, and when not on a diet tends to lean a little toward chubby. He had on a total-body sheep costume of curly faux fur, complete with a headpiece that he tied under his chin. His nose was even painted black. He looked like Richard Simmons on acid. He looked like a cotton ball that had been shoved into a light socket. He looked like he was the crazy, gone-wrong entertainment at a kids' party. He looked like . . . oh, you get it.

Shana Stern, on the other hand, was an old pro. An ex-Playmate, she obviously had been to the mansion many, many times. She was wearing a barely there devil outfit. So were about fifty other women. Bobbing up and down across the lawn was a sea of devil horns. I didn't know devils wore thongs, but apparently they do at Hef's parties. Shana was in her midforties, but, God bless her, she could still pull it off. Tasteful? I'm not so sure. You know that saying: Just because you can doesn't mean you should!

"Well, I'm glad you guys could make it! And, George, you've outdone yourself. But couldn't you have toned it down a bit? Look around! There aren't a lot of gay guys here. At least none that are out of the closet."

"Honey, this place has seen it all, but they've never seen the likes of me. I figured go *baa* or go home."

"Thanks for inviting us, Shana. This'll be fun," I said.

Shana was the ex-wife of Barry Stern, an actor on my show, *The Bare and the Brazen*. We had seen each other at events and parties over the years, but we were only passing acquaintances. That's why I had been surprised when I'd received an e-mail from her inviting me to this party. I needed a girls' night out, since I had been concentrating on my six-year-old daughter, Sarah, just about 24/7 for a good while, so I said yes. I had mixed feelings, however. Shana had a reputation for having a bit of an inner diva, but I decided, What the hell? She couldn't be that bad, right?

"Let's go get hammered!" Shana said. She grabbed my hand and I grabbed George's, uh, hoof, and off we went.

Chapter 2

As we entered the massive foyer of the Playboy Mansion, we saw every kind of costume imaginable. *Sexy* was the name of the game and there was no shortage of bare flesh, even if originality was lacking. Most of the women were angels, devils, maids, fairies or nymphs.

Shana dragged me through the house and outside to the backyard, which was the size of a football field. It was covered completely by a massive tent.

"Ow! Watch where you're going!"

"Sorry!" My stiff crinoline had taken out some guy, but it wasn't just any guy—it was actor Matthew Perry. And he was chatting with talk-show guy Bill Maher. Neither looked at each other while they talked. Probably scoping out the hundreds of women. I couldn't fault them, though. This place was very distracting, with its four-to-one ratio of women to men. *Naked* women to *clothed* men.

Music pounded from the multitude of speakers. Four girls dressed only in body paint were dancing on the stage in cages.

"Oh, my God! That's Paris Hilton!" George gasped.

I turned, and sure enough, Paris had jumped up on the stage and was doing an impromptu cage dance.

"Wow, she looks . . . cute." In a fairy costume. Of course.

As we were approaching one of five bars on the premises, we heard, "Miss Stern? Miss Stern?" A strange-looking man pushed a beautifully wrapped gift basket into Shana's arms.

"Oh, sweet Jesus! Not that asshole again. Security!" Shana yelled. Loudly.

"Wait! Miss Sternnnn! I need to speak with you. I just want to speak with youuu."

His voice was very low, and he had a weird and off-putting way of talking. His hair was frizzy and unkempt. On top of that, he seemed to be squinting with his left eye, giving him the appearance of a deranged pirate. He held up his camera phone. Real cameras were strictly banned from Hef's parties.

"Who is this guy, Shana?" I asked. "He seems a little weird." I was being kind. He was a *lot* weird.

"What the hell do you think? He's a stalker! I've been getting ten letters a week from him for the past two years. He's not supposed to be anywhere near me!" As she spoke, she put me in between herself and the man. Having had my own share of psycho stalkers, I was nervous, so I grabbed George and used him as a buffer.

"Hey, missy . . . I know what you're do—" Before George could finish his sentence, two extremely buff security guards jogged up.

"Sorry, Miss Stern. We don't know how he got in!" the tall blond one said.

"But that's your job, isn't it?" she berated them. "Aren't you supposed to know these things? Aren't you called *security* exactly for that reason?"

I understood Shana was upset, but she was coming down on the guys a little too hard.

"Perhaps they should call you *morons*. Would that be more appropriate?"

The security guards didn't look too happy, especially since people had started to gather around. It was embarrassing.

"I need to speeeeeak with you," the stalker whined. "You need to know about Genesis 1:27. Genesis 1:27." He was still trying to take a photo of her even as he was being led away.

This wasn't just your garden-variety stalker. Shana had gotten herself the classic Bible-quoting stalker. I was surprised he wasn't warning all of us about Sodom and Gomorrah, considering where we were.

"There are so many weirdos in the world and too many idiots. Now I really need a drink!" Shana said as she dumped the gift basket into the closest trash bin.

"Hey, Greenie! Three shots of tequila, with salt and lime. Make mine a double. And don't take too long!" Shana shouted to the bartender. He was dressed as the Incredible Hulk and had the muscles to back it up. He gave her a look, then turned away to get the drinks. Her inner diva wasn't so inner anymore.

"Shana! Don't be so mean! He's cute." George

said. "I like his tat." I looked and saw a huge eye tattooed on the bartender's right bicep. "Did you get that on *LA Ink*?" The bartender looked at George but didn't say anything. "Just want to make sure you keep an *eye* on me? *Haaaa!*"

I turned to face Shana.

"Shana, I know the stalker thing can be upsetting, but you don't have to be so rude. And a double? Isn't that a little hard-core?" I asked quietly.

I finally got a good look at her. I hadn't seen Shana in a couple of years. It was clear that time hadn't been very kind to her. She looked a little rough around the edges. Like she'd been living a hard life. Maybe she had a drinking problem. I could tell from her demeanor it wasn't the first shot she'd ordered that night.

Shana ignored me. "Hey, George." She was slurring. "Could you pleashe go and check out the grotto? It'sh over there behind the buffet. That'sh where everyone uzsually ends up naked at around three a.m. See if anyone is starting early, huh?"

George looked at me with a raised eyebrow, knowing he was being brushed off. I shrugged.

"Sure, honey. I'll be right back. Save me that shot."

George and I exchanged a glance, and off he went, wagging his tail behind him. I wondered for the umpteenth time whether that costume was really his idea, or his life partner, Wayne's—some wicked form of revenge. I'd have to ask Wayne the next time I saw him.

"What's going on with you?" I asked her. The bartender laid down the three shots, and Shana tossed back her double without hesitation. The movement caused her to stagger.

"Whoa, take it easy." I put my arm around her. "Are you okay?"

"You have no idea what it'sh like, Alex. No idea. I can't talk to anyone. And I mean anyone. You think I ashked you here just as a friendly invitation?" She brushed away a strand of bleached blond hair that had gotten stuck in her lip gloss. "I've got a big problem. I didn't know who elshe to talk to. All these years, I've seen you at parties. Umm, you seem nice. You know, normal?" Now, that might be a stretch, but I guess everything is relative.

"Well, sure, Shana. If you're having a problem, I'm happy to talk to you. Is it about that stalker? I do have some experience dealing with guys like him."

"No! It'sh not about that stupid jerk." She spit the *J* in my face. I flinched. "Just listen. I know your boyfriend is a cop, right?" She was referring to Detective Frank Jakes. *Boyfriend* always sounds strange at this stage of life, but he was a boy and he was my friend. Oh, whatever.

"Yeah, he's a detective with the LAPD. Why? Are you in trouble?"

"It's more than that. Much more." She was really nervous and kept looking over her shoulder, sucking on her lower lip.

"Okay, soooo . . . ?"

Before she could answer, a very tall redheaded

wood nymph or fairy interrupted us. I would guess she was a wood nymph. She had leaves strategically placed on her green-painted body, and a head covered with leaves and flowers. Maybe she was a tree branch. Or a green tomato worm.

"Shana! There's a photographer taking pictures of all the Playmates from the eighties in the dining room. You were Miss September 1986. We need you!"

"Oh, for Christ's sake. Just do it without me. Can't you? I'm busy!" Shana snapped. "I'm talkin' to someone."

"You don't have to be so mean." Wood Nymph seemed hurt. "We need you. We have all the girls from 'eighty-six but you. It's important to Hef."

"Like Hef could give a shit!" Shana clearly didn't want to go. She took George's shot and tossed it down the hatch. Jeez, she could drink. But could she stand?

"I'll be right back and I'll tell you . . . everything." She had a crazed look in her eyes. She pointed her finger at me and again said, "I'll be right back! Twenty minutes or so. Okay? Right back."

She took her fingers and plumped up her teased hair, licked her lips and put on a well-worn Playmate pout. She and the wood nymph made their way through the crowd on their wobbly stilettos, heading back toward the mansion. I didn't know then that Shana's fanny, covered in red fishnet pantyhose, would be the last I'd ever see of her . . . alive.

Chapter 3

"Where's Shana? And, more important, where's my shot?" George was back and he looked a little sweaty.

"She had to do a quick photo op and took your shot with her. What happened to you, anyway?"

"That grotto is steamy. I'm not sure if it's the hot water or all the naked people." He wiped his forehead with a cocktail napkin. "And how rude is that Shana? I mean, really? Really?"

"Don't take it personally. Turns out she has something bad going on and is interested in talking to Jakes about it. She's going to explain when she gets back. Want another shot?"

"Honey, I want something more civilized. Helloooo! Mr. Bartender!" George waved over a bartender dressed as Zorro. "Where's my Incredible Hulk? Oh, never mind. He was a snob. Nice pants, BTW. Cosmopolitan, please. Not so sweet . . . sweetie."

George caught the look I was giving him.

"What? All this blatant heterosexuality brings out my inner Liberace. Now what do we do?"

"Well, we wait for Shana." I made a face. "Want to dance?"

We both looked out at the dance floor. Lots of girls dancing with girls, guys dancing with girls. No Bo Peeps dancing with their sheep, however.

"What the hell? Let's get our party on, girl!" George pushed me toward the dance floor.

I carefully made my way out into the crowd, trying unsuccessfully to avoid getting my high heels stuck in the grass. We found a spot and started shaking our groove things to some old-school disco. I was feeling kind of fabulous until my puffed-out skirt sideswiped a glass of champagne sitting on a nearby table. It went flying and landed on a guy dressed as a corpse. His hands had been all over a woman who appeared to be a good fifty years younger. I looked closer. He wasn't dressed as a corpse. He was just *really* old. And he didn't look too happy. I grabbed George.

"Let's get out of here. I'm too dangerous!"

"Where to, Miss Bo Peep?"

We looked at each other. "The haunted house!" we said in unison.

I'm a big lover of being scared. I mean *safe scared*. The kind where you know it's not real. I'd had my share of the real kind the past couple of years, and fake fear is better. George is always game for fun, so off we went.

We wended our way past the grotto, another bar and the buffet, being careful not to knock any grilled shrimp kebabs off the table with my skirt. After passing a dozen or so of the Porta Potties set up for the party and an area set aside for the two smokers left in Los Angeles, we ended up on the expansive front lawn. Smack-dab in front of the haunted house.

A blanket of fake fog covered the ground and crept up the walls of the newly erected building. Screams emanated from inside. There were only a few people in line, so our timing couldn't have been better.

"Nice outfits." A pimp and his hooker were looking George and me up and down. I assumed they were in costume, but who knew?

"Thanks," I managed to say as we shuffled ahead with the line.

A couple of angels were behind us now, giggling as their boobs tried to make a run for it out of their skimpy costumes. As we got closer, I started to get excited. And nervous.

"I love this, Georgie! Now, don't be a baby. Don't scream and don't grab me. Man up. Okay?"

"Yes, honey. Don't you worry about me," George assured me.

Finally we were in. It was pitch-black, but I could make out something large looming up ahead. I started to sweat.

"Ahhhh!" I screamed. I couldn't help it. A mummy grabbed me. We were shuffling through a very narrow hallway. It opened up into a small room where a bikini-clad girl was tied to a table and slowly being tortured by Leatherface. You know, *The Texas Chainsaw Massacre* guy. As we hugged the farthest wall, a hand reached out and grabbed my leg.

"Ahhhhh!" Okay, sorry. It was me screaming again.

"Whatever happened to *man up*, Alex? You're hurting me!"

"I'm not touching you, George!" He looked behind him.

"Ahhh! Run!" A big, bloody guy with an ax protruding from his head had George by the tail.

We tried to pick up the pace, but we kept bumping into the people ahead of us. It was very discombobulating because we couldn't see anything. Screams came from the hall in front of us. Then we were in another room.

This one was the famous *Psycho* scene. Janet Leigh in the shower, being knifed. I have to say, they did a great job. The blood, or food-colored corn syrup that passes for blood, looked very real. The girl screamed as she was knifed through the shower curtain. The killer had a maniacal look on his face.

Again we were shoved forward. Pitch-black, screams getting ever louder. Someone grabbed me from behind.

"George, is that you?" I yelled. No answer. I slowly turned and found myself face-to-face with the guy from *Scream*. And so I did.

"Ahhh!" I took off running as fast as I could, but stumbled over a rug.

"Owww!" It wasn't a rug; it was George.

"What the hell are you doing down there? Get up."

"Oh, just resting! What do you mean? I was pushed. Alex, seriously. I want out of here. This is crazy!"

We continued pushing forward until the hallway opened up to a dimly lit room. It was Michael Myers, and he had yet another barely dressed woman lying on the floor under him, and his ax came swinging down on her. She was screaming bloody murder. Did I detect a theme here? This was bringing the term *torture porn* to a whole new level. Did any males get chopped up in Hef's haunted house? I was about to make a political statement about misogynists and the world when George yelled.

"Let's get out of here. Now!"

He pushed me into the next hallway murder room. I heard a door close and then there was complete silence. It felt as if the air had been sucked out of the room. And my lungs. And then I heard a repetitive *squeak . . . squeak . . . squeak.*

I looked around the corner, holding my breath. George was squeezing the life out of my arm. And then I saw it. A little tricycle going around and around in circles. It was being ridden by a mechanized doll of some kind. As he rode around to face me, I realized it was the creepy little clown from the *Saw* series. Then he steered toward a chair where yet another half-naked woman sat. A horrible torture device was attached to her bloody head, and a pool of blood grew around her feet.

"George, look." I whispered. "That puddle is actually getting bigger. How do they make the fake blood do that?" We stepped a little closer.

"Alex. That's Shana!" George was amused. "Hey, sweetie. So this is where you've been? I hope you're getting paid a lot. All that corn syrup in your hair. You better get that nasty stuff out right away or—"

"Georgie, shut up!" Something wasn't right. I stepped even closer and looked at her eyes. Maybe she'd passed out from all the alcohol.

"Shana, you okay?" There was no response. I touched her, and then I knew. Quickly backing up, I grabbed George.

"George, call the police. Shana's dead!"

Chapter 4

Within a half hour, the party was suddenly taken over by the color blue—police uniforms. They had responded when called and immediately requested more help to secure the scene and shut the party down so nobody could leave. As Detective Frank Jakes walked over, followed by his partner, Detective Len Davis, he barked at a couple of men who were ogling the Playboy centerfolds. Couldn't blame them, really. After all, they were men.

Jakes was taking me in as he approached us. He had that kind of dopey look on his face he got sometimes. Happy to see me, but more than that. My heart skipped a beat. He obviously wanted to hug me or something, but was on the job. We kind of hovered near each other. God knows I could have used a hug. It looked like Georgie could use one, too. He was very pale.

"Okay," Jakes said to me, "let me have it. How did you manage to find another body?"

I looked pointedly at him.

"Shana is . . . was a friend of mine. Sort of . . ."

I wrapped my arms around Georgie, who was shaking.

"Sorry. I didn't mean to seem insensitive. It's just . . . kind of uncanny."

Jakes was right. I seemed to attract dead bodies like flies to poop. I jumped right in.

"Shana had a stalker approach her tonight." That really got his attention.

"What happened? Exactly." Jakes moved in a little closer.

"We were standing at the bar when this guy came up to her with a gift basket," I answered. "She freaked and had him thrown out."

"Did she call him by name? What did he look like? Can you remember anything that stands out about him?"

"I think she referred to him as "asshole," but that's about it. He was very strange. I mean, if you were to look up *stalker* in the dictionary, you'd probably see his face. And, oh yeah, he had a squinty eye."

Jakes looked up from his notes with an odd expression on his face.

"What? He did!" I said. "And crazy hair, too. He had a weird way of speaking—he kept drawing out his wordsssssss. Like thisssssss."

"Well, okay. So he sounded odd and he looked odd. Did he seem threatening?"

"No. I mean, Shana didn't seem scared, just very annoyed. As he was being dragged away he kept yelling a Bible quote. Something from Genesis, I think." Then something came to me. "She definitely knew him. I mean, she said he was a longtime stalker of hers."

"She was royally pissed off at the security guys when they came over and took him away. I mean, really belittled them. It was humiliating." George said.

"Why's that?" Jakes looked at George.

"Apparently, there had been strict orders to keep him off the premises," George said. "He got in anyway. She was over-the-top rude, if you ask me."

Jakes took this in, then asked, "Where's the gift basket now?"

"Uh, she dumped it in a trash can by the bar when the guy was dragged away. I'll show you." George started toward the bar.

Jakes told two of his men to follow George and collect the basket.

"And be careful with it. We need to process it for prints." Jakes saw that Len Davis had now joined the boys in blue in ogling the Playmates. Jakes backhanded him on the chest.

"Pay attention, Len."

"I am payin' attention," he said. Jakes rolled his eyes.

"Okay, Alex, tell me what happened in the haunted house before we take a look at the body."

"It's pretty straightforward, really," I said. "It's set up with scenes from famous slasher movies. We found Shana in the *Saw* room, dead."

"What's *Saw*?" Jakes asked. "Is that like a chain saw?" Clearly he didn't get out much.

"*Saw* is a hugely successful horror-movie franchise. Ever hear of torture porn?"

He looked at me blankly.

"Okay, well, it's an over-the-top gory movie."

"And Shana is your friend how?"

"She's the ex-wife of Barry Stern, an actor on my show. She and I have seen each other over the years at different events and things. We weren't really friends, per se. But we were friend*ly*."

"'Eighty-six, right?" Davis asked.

"What?" Jakes said.

Davis was looking at me. "She was a Playmate in 'eighty-six, right?"

"How do you know that?"

"Don't ask," Jakes said. "You'll only lose respect—*more* respect—for him. Okay, take us to it."

"To what?"

"The body. Do you think you can handle it?" he said.

"You want me to go back in there with you?" I asked.

"Yeah," Jakes said, then looked at George, who had just returned from the bar. "Both of you. I mean, it could help us find the killer or killers." Then to George, "Did you find the basket?"

"Yeah, right on top where she tossed it. Do I really have to go back in there?" George looked like he was going to cry.

"They need us, George. Shana needs us. You can do it." I put my arm around him.

"Oh. I don't know." Georgie said, looking from

me to Jakes and back again. "I guess I could try. What if I have to hurl?"

"It wouldn't be the first time. C'mon." And off George and I went for a second go-round at the haunted house, with Jakes and Davis closely behind.

All the lights were on in the haunted house, making it easy to retrace our steps. Along the way we passed more uniformed cops. The mansion was in complete lockdown, with cops at every conceivable exit. I wondered how Hef was taking it.

". . . and then we came to . . . here," I said as we turned the corner. I was having a difficult time looking at the display. George groaned. There were two uniformed cops standing watch over Shana's body, so Jakes didn't really need us to take him to it.

"Is this exactly the way it was?" Jakes asked.

I peeked through my hands. Shana was still there, still dead, but something was different.

"The tricycle," I said.

"What about it?"

"It was going around and around, squeaking."

Jakes looked at the two uniforms who were standing guard over the scene.

"Who turned that bike off?"

The men exchanged a glance, and then one of them said, "The squeaking was driving us nuts."

Jakes stood toe to toe with the man and read his name tag.

"Officer Reardon, in the future, you don't touch a thing at the scene of a homicide—especially if it's my case." He jabbed the younger man in the chest with a rigid forefinger. "You got that?"

"Yes, sir," the officer said tightly.

"How about you, Officer Webb? You got that?"

"I got it, sir."

"Now, did you geniuses turn anything else on or off?" Davis asked. "Touch anything else?"

"No, sir," Webb said. "We did not."

"Okay," Davis said.

As he and Jakes put on some latex surgical gloves, Jakes looked at George and me and said, "You two stand right there and don't move. We can't have this scene contaminated any further."

I felt bad for Shana. She was barely wearing any clothing. She seemed so vulnerable. Exposed. I knew she was dead. But still.

"Could we cover her with a blanket or something?" I asked.

"In a minute." Jakes said as the two of them approached Shana's body, then leaned over to get a closer look. I noticed the blood on the floor was still very wet, and drops still fell from Shana's body.

"Maybe somebody just had enough of her." I stepped over next to him.

"What do you mean?" Jakes looked at me.

"Shana had a reputation. I heard things about her. And I saw her in action tonight. She wasn't very nice to people. The security guards can tell you. She gave divas a bad name."

Jakes took it in and then looked down.

"She's bled out," he said.

"How long does it take a body to do that?" I asked.

"Depending on the artery that's severed," Jakes said, "could be minutes; could even be seconds. What's dripping now isn't coming from her. It's dripping from beneath her."

"She was still bleeding when we found her," I said.

"Are you sure about that?"

"Yes. I even commented on how realistic the whole thing looked," I said as I glanced over at George. He seemed dangerously close to tossing his cookies.

"I gotta get outta here, guys. It's really hot." George scratched at his collar.

"Well," Jakes said, "the ME should be arriving any minute, and we'll have too many people in here when he does." He looked at the two officers. "Webb, please walk Alex and George outside, will you? Stay there until the ME gets here with his men, then bring them all in."

"Yessir." He walked up to us. "Let's go, folks."

"Thanks, you two. I know this wasn't an easy thing to do." Jakes stood closer to me. "Are you okay?"

"Yeah, I-I'm okay." Actually, I thought I was going to faint. I took a few deep breaths and the feeling passed. "I still need to talk to you, but I have to get Georgie out of here." I said. "I'm feeling a little light-headed myself. Do you ever get used to it? The dead-body thing?" I asked him.

"Yes. And no. Get some fresh air." He squeezed my hand.

"There's something else I need to tell you . . . about Shana. I don't know what it means, but I think it may be . . . something." I reached out for him to steady myself. "Sorry—I'm such a lightweight. I feel . . . a little woozy."

"It's okay. You are a civilian, you know. It's a lot to take in. Go get some air, and I'll come find you when I'm through in here. We can talk then."

"Okay."

I turned to George to tell him we were leaving, but he was already falling, fainting dead away.

Chapter 5

Officer Webb caught George before he hit the ground. He and another officer escorted us outside, where we were besieged with questions. The two most popular were "What happened?" and "When can we leave?" George was in no condition to answer either one, and I started throwing out "No comment" here and there.

"You'll have to ask the detective in charge," I told them.

"So, what do we do now?" George asked, taking deep breaths. We found two chairs. The officers lowered him into one and went back inside. I struggled with my petticoats.

"Put your head between your legs if you still feel dizzy," I told him. "It will pass. I promise." I wasn't feeling so hot, either, so I bent over. "We'll just have to do what everybody else is doing," I said. "Wait."

"But you have an in." He sounded muffled from between his haunches. "You could get us out of here."

"We're not going to get out of here early. We

found the body. Besides, don't you want to help find out who killed her? We owe Shana that much. Why don't you take your costume off?"

Strange but true, we were having a conversation from between our respective legs at the Playboy Mansion. Just when you thought life couldn't get any weirder.

"I would," he grumbled, "but I have nothing on underneath."

"George," I said, sitting upright, "you went commando?"

"I knew it would be hot." He wriggled his shoulders. "Itches like hell."

Poor George. But I still didn't want to ask Jakes for special treatment. Especially considering all the grief he had taken for being involved with me to begin with.

Right at that moment, my cell rang. It was small enough that I had been able to tuck it beneath my costume. I dug it out, checked the readout and then closed it.

"Connie again?" he asked.

I nodded. My manager, Connie, had called several times while we were in the car on the way to the party.

"Not going to answer?" he asked.

"She's still trying to talk me into going to Daytime in the Desert."

"Why don't you? Those are your fans."

"I know," I said, "but those things wear me out."

Daytime in the Desert was a fan event involving

the two longest-running soaps on TV—*The Bare and the Brazen* and my old show, *The Yearning Tide*. Two days of appearances, signings, parties—the works. It made me tired just thinking of it.

"I see high heels approaching," George said, as I tucked away my cell again.

I turned and saw one of Hef's blondes heading for us. She was wearing an angel outfit, of course.

"Are you Alex?" she asked. "They told me to look for Little Miss Muffet."

"It's Little Bo Peep, actually, and yes, I am."

"Oh, funny!" She looked at George, who was sitting upright now, more or less. "I get it! Bo Peep and her sheep! Ha ha! Anywayyyy, Hef would like to talk to you, if you're not busy."

"Not busy. Where should I go?"

"Follow me," she said.

I stood up, fighting my petticoats again.

"Bringing your sheep?" she asked.

"George?"

"I think I'll just sit here and wait," he said. "This lamb's hooves are hurting a little."

"Where this Little Bo Peep goes," I said to the girl, "her sheep doesn't necessarily follow."

"That's funny!" she exclaimed again. "I just love lambs. They're so cute, aren't they? White and fluffy! So cute!"

I followed the girl's flat, skinny butt into the mansion. She could use a little more junk in her trunk, if you know what I mean. A few Twinkies and Ding

Dongs would be a good place to start. From the foyer, we turned the corner into the dining room. Hef was sitting with another angel, a devil, a cat and a wood nymph around a grand dining room table. For a second I thought it was the same nymph that took Shana to the photo shoot. Then I realized she was a brunette.

"You're Alex?" he asked, taking the pipe from his mouth. "Thanks for coming." Hef got up to greet me, straightening his silk bathrobe.

"No problem," I said. "We can't leave anyway. You know, we met years ago. In the eighties. I was here a couple of times."

"Ahhh. The eighties. Those were good times." He looked me up and down. "I'm surprised you weren't in the magazine. Did we ask you to pose?"

"Uh, yes. It just didn't feel right at the time. Ha! It's probably too late now, right?" I said, joking. There was a slightly awkward pause.

"Can I get you something?" he said, circumventing the question.

"No, thanks," I said. "I'm fine. There's still plenty of food and drink out there."

"I thought it best to keep the buffets and bars open," he said. "People might as well be able to eat and drink if they can't leave."

The eyes of all the girls were on me, and I felt silly in my costume. Unlike George, I did have something on underneath, but it was just a bra and panties.

"Was there something you wanted to ask me?"

"I understand you found Shana," he said.

"That's right."

"Can you tell me anything?" he asked. "I'm in the dark here. And I can't say I like it very much."

I told him what George and I had found. All the girls around him put their hands over their mouths as I described what I had seen.

"Poor Shana. She was family." He wiped a tear from his eye.

The thing you had to love about Hef was that he considered every girl who ever appeared in *Playboy* magazine his family. I'm sure he'd felt it deeply when Anna Nicole Smith died, and now he was feeling Shana's death, as well.

"Who would do that to her?" he asked. "And why do it here? During the party? Seems to me that was taking a hell of a chance."

"Maybe it wasn't planned," I said. "Maybe somebody just saw an opportunity to kill her."

"But why?"

"That's for the police to find out." Something occurred to me just then. "Did she make it to the photo shoot?"

"What photo shoot?"

"A girl came over to us and told Shana that you wanted her for a photo shoot of all the Playmates from the eighties," I said.

"I wanted her?" he asked. "I don't know anything about that." He looked around at his girls, who all shook their heads.

"I wonder why someone would want just girls from the eighties?" he asked.

That question had not occurred to me earlier. Now that I realized Shana had been lured away with a lie, I felt foolish for not having asked it.

"She didn't actually mention you," I said, remembering. "She said a photographer wanted her."

"Well, there are plenty of them around," he said.

"Can you ask if any of them had that idea?"

"Of course."

"I'll tell the detective in charge you're doing that," I said. But first I had to get rid of my damn petticoats.

Chapter 6

I took off my crinoline, flattened my skirt, ripped off a few bows and buttons and then went to find Jakes. But I ran into George instead, right where I'd left him.

"Oh, fine," he said, jumping to his feet, "Bo Peep's gone, and now I just look like a fool in sheep's clothing."

"And now I look like Daisy Mae. Do you still want to barf?"

"No. I feel a little better. But we've got to get out of here, Alex," George said. "I'm melting."

"I'm looking for Jakes now," I said. "I'll see what he says."

"Thank you." He sat back down. "I'm going to wait right here."

I nodded and headed over to the haunted house. The boys in blue were still keeping the curious away.

"Is Jakes still inside?" I asked one of them.

"Detective Jakes? Yeah, he's in there, wrapping things up. It should be a few more minutes."

*   *   *

Not exactly. More than a little while later, I called my mother to tell her what had happened and that I didn't know when I'd be getting home. As I was disconnecting the call, I saw the ME's men wheel the body out on a gurney, followed by the ME himself and then, finally, Jakes and Davis. I waved. Jakes said something to Davis and came over.

"Her throat was cut," he told me. "ME says she would have bled out in seconds."

"Poor Shana." I grimaced.

"Where's Hefner?" Jakes asked. "I should talk to him, since we've locked down his party."

"He's up at the manse," I said, "but I've got something to tell you first."

"Sounds important." He took me by the elbow and walked me away from the haunted house. "What is it, Alex?"

I told him how Shana had invited me to the party so she could talk to me about something, but just as we were going to get into it, a woman came over and called her away. Next time I saw Shana, she was dead.

"So you have no idea why she wanted to see you?"

"None," I said. "All I know is she said she had nobody else she could talk to."

"So some girl called her away to a phony photo shoot with a nonexistent photographer?"

"That's what I'm having Hef find out," I said.

"Okay, so," Jakes said, "who was the woman?"

"I don't know."

"What do you mean?" he asked, confused. "Didn't you talk to her?"

"Not really. I've been looking around for her, but she was dressed as a wood nymph or wood fairy or something. Painted head to toe in green. You'd be surprised how many girls have on a similar costume."

"Oh, come on. It can't be that difficult. How many wood nymphs could there be?"

"Are you kidding? Have you looked around?"

Right on cue, a winged fairy walked by. But she was head to toe in blue. I nodded toward her, making a *See, I told you so* face as she sauntered by.

"Okay. I get your point. Maybe she's at the mansion. Let's go on up. You can introduce me to Mr. Hefner."

Chapter 7

Jakes didn't allow Davis to come into the mansion with us. Instead, Davis was in charge of making sure everyone at the party was interviewed, and collecting names and addresses.

"He's not only a soap opera fanatic," he told me, "he's a *Playboy* fanatic, too. I can't trust him around these girls."

"And can you trust yourself?" I asked.

"Of course," he said. "I've got a girl of my own who puts all of them to shame."

I hip bumped him and said, "Good answer, baby."

Hef was in the same room where I'd left him, but the ladies were elsewhere. It was just Hef, Jakes and me.

"Hef, this is Detective Jakes. He's the man in charge."

"Detective," Hef said, shaking hands with Jakes, "thanks very much for the prompt response."

"Just trying to do our job," Jakes said. "The body has been removed, and we're questioning guests as we speak."

"When can we let people go home?" Hef asked.

"Not for a while, I'm afraid," Jakes said. "Everybody who attended the party has to be considered a suspect. We're also going to need help finding out who left before we arrived and locked the place down. We're taking everybody's names and addresses now, and we'll need your guest list to compare it to."

"I'll have Mary get it to you right away. She's in charge of basically everything here. Anything else?"

"Yes," Jakes said. "Alex last saw Shana Stern at about ten o'clock, and then found her body close to eleven. What were you doing between ten and eleven?"

Hef's eyebrows went up.

"I'm a suspect?"

"As I said," Jakes answered, "we're questioning everybody."

"Well, I was mingling with the guests," Hef said.

"Do you remember which guests in particular you spoke to during that time?"

"No," Hef said. "There are a lot of people here. The best I can do is let you talk to the girls who were with me. Maybe they'd remember who we spoke to."

"How many girls?"

"Five."

"You had five girls with you while you were mingling?" Jakes asked.

"Yes."

"At all times?"

"Pretty much," Hef said.

Jakes looked at me.

"Pretty good alibi, huh?" I asked.

"I'd say so." Jakes looked at Hef. "I'll need to speak to those, uh, five women, too."

"Of course," Hef said. "Now?"

"If possible."

"I thought you might want to talk to me alone, but I'll bring them in here."

"Thanks."

"Be right back."

"Okay."

Hef walked out of the room, leaving me and Jakes alone.

"So this is the mansion?"

"You've never been here before, huh?" I asked.

"As far as I know, nobody's been murdered here while I've been with homicide."

"Actually," I said, "nobody's been murdered here now. Technically, that is."

"Right," Jakes said. "She was killed in the haunted house, which is, I believe, a temporary structure."

"Right. He puts it up every year for the Halloween party."

"Someone must have taken her in by a back entrance," Jakes said. "The killer wouldn't want to be seen going in the front."

"But it's Halloween. They would have had a costume on. Nobody would have recognized them, anyway."

"True. And that's going to make things even more

difficult. Alex, you've got to try to remember which girl called Shana away from you."

"George! Of course! He might remember! Should I go get him?" I said.

"Wait on that. Stay here with me and see if you recognize one of Hef's entourage. If you don't, then go get George."

"Sure. You probably just want protection from these wild Playmates."

"Well, that, too." He looked around to see if anyone was watching and snuck in a quick kiss.

Chapter 8

The girls were brought in one by one. Hef had left the room, but I was still there. Even so, two of the girls flirted outrageously with Jakes while they answered his questions. I had to restrain myself from having a slap fight with one of them, who kept pushing her boobs in his face.

But in the end, all the girls alibied Hef and themselves. None of them knew anything about a photographer shooting eighties Playmates.

"Can I do anything else?" Hef asked.

"I'd like to know who constructed the haunted house for you," Jakes said, "and who was around when it was finished."

"Sure," Hef said. "We have it built by the same people each year. I'll get you a card."

When we left the mansion, Jakes had the business card in his pocket. He hadn't shown it to me, but I figured I'd get a look at it later.

I told him I couldn't pick the girl out from any in the mansion.

"So you're saying you didn't recognize her from that group, or you can't recognize her at all?"

I hesitated, and then said, "It wasn't that wood nymph. I'm positive of that. The one that got Shana was taller—and, now that I think of it, she was older."

Jakes sighed and looked around.

"I've got to find Len, make sure the body's been removed from the premises. And I want to take another look around. Why don't you get George; let's meet up in a half hour."

"Where?" I asked.

"You tell me. You've been here before, right?"

"The grotto," I said. "Let's meet there."

"Okay." He touched my arm, started away, then stopped and turned. "You *have* been here before, right?"

"A few times."

"Were you, uh, ever in the magazine?"

I couldn't help it. "I was, actually."

He stared at me, started to say something, then shook his head and walked away. From his expression, I figured he was about to ask if I'd been in the magazine naked.

Let him ask, I thought, and went off to find Georgie.

When I found him, he had managed to get his head and feet off. It didn't look as if he'd gotten any relief, though. His face was wet with perspiration, and his hair was matted and damp. He was wearing support socks that went almost to his knees.

"Oh, thank God," he said. "Can we go now?"

"Not quite yet." I told him I couldn't remember the wood nymph who came to get Shana for an apparently phony photo shoot. "There are just so many of them around here. . . ."

"Oh, I could pick her out."

"You could?"

"Honey," he said, rolling his eyes, "that hair . . . She needed a gallon of conditioner. That frizz factor! Oh, my God! If I had just had her in my chair—"

I grabbed his hand and pulled him to his feet.

"Hey!"

"Come on, Georgie," I said. "You may have just earned your ticket home."

Chapter 9

"It's none of them."

Jakes and I glared at George, who got very defensive.

"Hey, don't look at me that way," he said. "You showed me five nymphs, and she isn't one of them."

"Okay," Jakes said, "that's okay, George. All we have to do now is walk you around the grounds until you spot her."

"What?" George looked at me. "You said I could go home after this."

Jakes looked at me. "You said that?"

"I said *maybe*." I turned from Jakes to George. "I said *maybe*, George."

"I'm melting!" George complained.

I looked at Jakes.

"What if I get Mr. Hefner to let you take a shower and I get you a change of clothes?" Jakes asked.

George didn't look happy.

"It's the best I can do, George," Jakes said apologetically. "You're our only reliable witness."

"I guess I should have kept my big mouth shut."

George looked at us. "I'm just kidding. Of course I want to help!" And then, glumly, "Okay, get me a shower."

Jakes managed to get a bathing suit and Hawaiian shirt that fit George. And some flip-flops.

"Better than the sheep costume," I said when he came down.

"Not by much." He looked down, clearly irritated at the pastel bathing suit, shirt and flip-flops. "This really isn't me."

"I like it," Jakes said.

George gave him a dubious look. "Don't tell me you're one of them? Straight guys who think all gays like pink and Barbra Streisand?"

Before Jakes could reply, George smiled. "I'm just kidding."

Jakes looked relieved. Before either of them could say anything else, Hef came in.

"Hey, they fit," he said to George. "Looks good."

"Thank you," George said politely.

"I don't think Jack will mind."

"Jack?" George asked.

"Nicholson," Hef said. "He usually wears those when he's here."

"Really?" George asked. "Jack Nicholson?"

"Uh-huh."

George looked down at himself again, and Hef took that moment to wink at me. I grinned back.

"Well, I guess I don't look so bad," George said, looking up and grinning at all of us.

"So, we can go outside now?" Jakes asked.

"Sure," George said. "I'm ready."

"And you're sure you'll be able to recognize her?" Jakes asked as they walked out.

"If I don't see her," George said, "then she's not here."

"Some party, huh, Alex?" Hef asked.

"It was," I said, "until Shana got killed. I'm so sorry, Hef."

"I'm sorry, too. Shana had an attitude sometimes, but she had a kind side and always loved a good party. And who knows? Maybe the party can go on after the police leave. Shana would have liked that."

He looked at me, and we both knew that wasn't going to happen.

I left Hef in the house and went outside. Some people were milling about; others were still being questioned by police, who were taking down names, addresses and phone numbers.

The party really was over.

Len Davis approached me and said, "Do you know where Jakes is?"

"He's walking around with George," I said, "looking for the girl who called Shana away."

He nodded.

"Are you ready to start letting people leave?" I asked.

"I'll have to ask Frank," he said. "It's his crime scene, but I think so."

"Hef will be happy to hear that."

"Hef, huh?" He looked at the mansion. As far as I knew, he hadn't been inside yet.

"Jakes is busy," I said. "I can take you inside and introduce you. You can tell Hef yourself."

"Inside?" he asked. He was trying not to seem eager. It was kind of cute in an I-get-to-meet-the-king-of-naked-women sort of way. "Sure, why not? Somebody's gotta keep him posted, right?"

I shrugged and said, "Might as well be you."

Chapter 10

"You're Len's hero, you know," Jakes said to me. We were in his car. He was driving me home from the party. We'd been there for hours. It was three a.m., and the cops had finally let people go home. I had told George to take the limo. He was disappointed that he hadn't ID'd the nymph.

I looked at Jakes. "You mean I made up for leaving *The Yearning Tide*?"

"Well," he said, "I don't know about that, but taking him into the mansion and introducing him to Hef sure earned you some points."

"I'm sorry about George."

"Don't worry," he said. "She got out somehow, before we had the place locked down."

"So, what do you think, Jakes?" I asked.

"Huh?"

"About who killed Shana? And why?"

"I was going to ask you that," he said. "After all, you knew her."

"Not that well."

"Well enough that when she needed someone to talk to, she turned to you."

"I think she only wanted to talk to me because I know you."

"You know who her friends were, right?"

"Sort of," I said. "I know her ex-husband. He's on my show." Then it dawned on me. "Are you asking me to help you with this investigation?"

He gave me a look before moving his eyes back to the road.

"Like I could keep you away?" he asked. "You're my ace assistant, right?"

He was right. I'd had a taste of being an amateur detective a couple of times before, and except for some bumps and bruises—and almost getting killed—had come out unscathed and oddly invigorated.

"I'll see what I can do for you, Detective."

"I knew I could count on you."

He pulled up in front of my house in Venice, one of those 1920s Craftsman types with the canal running behind it. I also had a smaller guesthouse back by the canal, where my mother lived. It was very handy, having her around to babysit my daughter, who was going to turn seven that year.

When we pulled up in front of the house, it was three thirty a.m. "Good night. Umm . . . we'll talk tomorrow?"

"Yeah. Of course. I understand, Alex." He leaned over to kiss me. He was *very* understanding about

Sarah being my priority. Jakes and I had actually been seeing each other for a year. But ever since I had broken up with my ex-boyfriend Paul, I had been very reticent to bring Jakes around my daughter. I didn't want to be one of those single moms who subjected their children to a merry-go-round of boyfriends. Making it even more difficult was the fact that Sarah and Paul had adored each other. My mother's being thrown into the equation only complicated things. She had been a big Paul fan, as well. What do you do when everyone else loves the guy but you? I had the feeling I was flunking this part of single parenthood, but I didn't quite know what to do. Was anybody winning?

Jakes could sense my conflict. He held my hand and looked at me. *Really* looked at me.

"I mean it, Alex. I do understand. I'm a grown-up." He brushed a ringlet away from my cheek. "I'll just miss you, that's all." He kissed me again.

"I'll miss you, too. Thanks." I was looking at the floor of the car, feeling a little inadequate.

"We'll figure this out, right?" I asked. He took my face in his hands and turned it toward him.

"Of course we will. *You're* worth it." I smiled at him, and he kissed me yet again. A slow, deep kiss that did crazy, thrilling things to me. It also reminded me why I was with him and not Paul. The windows of the car were getting a little steamed up when he broke away.

"I told you I was understanding, but I'm not superhuman. Go, before I throw you in the backseat."

I disentangled myself from his arms, smelled his neck one last time and got out of the car. I was heading toward the house and thought of something. "By the way, I lied." Jakes looked puzzled. "I was never really in the magazine."

He just shook his head and smiled as he drove away. I opened the front door quietly.

"Hey, Mom!" Sarah yelled. So I guess they were awake after all. I barely had time to set down my Bo Peep staff before she threw herself into my arms. "Where's Georgie?" she asked.

She had seen George in his sheep outfit when the limo had picked me up the previous evening.

"He had to go home and go to sleep," I said. "What are you doing up?"

She yawned. "I heard the phone ring when you called and I woke up. Was the party fun?"

"It was okay, sweetie," I said, kissing her cheek. "I'll tell you about it later."

My mother came into the living room, looking bleary-eyed in her pj's and hair curlers.

"How did it go?" she asked.

"Terrible," I said. I put Sarah down and said, "Honey, I'm going to take my makeup off and get my jams on. Go to bed, and I'll be in to snuggle. You need to get some more sleep."

"Okay, Mom. I'm super tired."

She yawned again and headed for her room.

"Poor Shana," I said. "It was horrible."

"Sweetheart, I really don't want to hear about it," my mother said, cutting me off, waving her hands.

"I hate the thought of you being involved in another murder."

"How do you know I'm involved?" I asked a little defensively.

She gave me a great deadpan look. "Was he there?"

"And by *he*, do you mean Detective Jakes?" I paused before finally surrendering. "Yes, Mom, he was."

"You're involved," she said as she walked out the back door toward her little guesthouse. "I'll see you in a couple of hours, honey. Get some sleep."

She left me standing there, feeling about six years old myself. How do moms do that? It's a special gift.

Chapter 11

I don't know what I expected people's reactions to be after the news of Shana's death made the rounds. I certainly didn't expect what I got at work the next day. Oh, they were shocked, of course, and a little sad—mostly for her ex, Barry. But people were sort of blasé, really. It made me feel very alone. Especially since George had texted me that he was staying home to "recuperate." I couldn't blame him. At least he was feeling something, right? Had our society devolved into one that celebrated violence so much that we were becoming immune to murder? Too many ultraviolent films and television shows? One too many celebrity murders? I'd like to think it was because people didn't know Shana that well. That's what I'd *like* to think, anyway.

Daytime television was going through lots of changes, and *The Bare and the Brazen* was no different. The show had begun to take drastic steps to save money. Sets were very expensive to put up and take down, so now the routine was to put up a set, like my character's living room, and in the same day film all the scenes from several episodes that took place there. It was more cost-effective, but it also meant you could spend all day at work just to tape three or four scenes from several different episodes. Not so great.

One thing that *was* great: I had plenty of time to make phone calls and talk to anyone who might have known Shana, including her ex.

The first thing I did when I got to hair and makeup was to ask whether Barry was in. No luck. It looked as if he wouldn't be in for quite a few days. He lived most of the time in Vegas and kept a small apartment in LA. I knew a few actors and actresses who had primary residences there and apartments in town. You could get a real deal on a huge house in a gated community in Vegas, and it was only an hour's flight. Still sounded like a pain.

No Barry today, so I asked around to see whether anyone had worked with Shana in the past few months on other shows or what have you. And sure enough, Patti Dennis had done Shana's makeup for a photo shoot just last month. Patti had been working on *The Bare and the Brazen* for thirty years. She started as a body makeup person and had worked her way up to head of the department. She also freelanced on occasion. Thus the shoot with Shana. Thankfully, she knew everything that was going on with the show, because everyone confided in her. But she wasn't a gossip. A rare breed.

"She did mention the stalker, but never mentioned his name." Patti gently brushed gray powder onto my eyelid.

"Did she actually *know* his name?" I asked, looking at her with one eye.

"I can't do your eyes when one is open. Close. I don't know," Patti said. "She used to say *that bastard* or *that son of a bitch*. If she knew his name, she never said it. But if you knew Shana, she referred to a lot of people that way. She was kind of a bi—" She stopped herself. The ugly head of integrity reared itself right when it was getting good. I gently tried to lead her on.

"I know Shana has, uh, had a reputation for being a bit of a diva. Did you ever find that to be true?"

"Oh, she was that, all right. Now close your eyes, or I'll poke you!" Patti clammed up, but somehow I had a very strong suspicion she knew something. I was afraid if I pushed too far, she'd never give it up, so I decided to retreat and find another tactic. I tried my sensitive side.

"I think Shana had a big problem. I mean, that's why she asked me to go to the party. I hardly knew her. Something must have really been troubling her for her to want to invite me. I really wish I knew what it was so I could at least help find her killer." I sincerely felt bad for Shana, so I even managed to tear up. I felt a little evil, too, for manipulating Patti.

"Oh, God! Don't do that! You'll ruin your makeup!" she cried.

But I could tell I had gotten to her. I kept going. "If you know something, it wouldn't be a betrayal of Shana's trust if you shared it with me. You never know what might prove helpful to the police. It could have been anything." I took a stab. "I don't know—maybe some problems with her ex?"

Bull's-eye! Patti looked troubled and started blinking a lot. She paused and said, "She and Barry *were* having some problems. Even though they were divorced, they had remained close. You know? But something happened to put a strain on their friendship." She paused, just a hair too long. "That's all I know!" She turned away to put her makeup brush down. "Okay. You're done! Who's doing your hair today with George out?"

I really didn't feel like sitting still for who knows how long.

"I'll just put it in a pony. No worries."

"Okay, then, you're good to go. And I have a department meeting upstairs!" Off she went, leaving me much prettier than when I first sat down, and much surer she was protecting someone.

I turned to the dressing-room sheet on the bulletin board behind me. Barry's room was 43B, but since he wasn't in today, that meant someone else was probably using his room. Luckily, it was Priscilla Schmidt; I knew she had finished her scenes and hopefully had even left the building.

I looked for a rubber band on the counter, gathered up my hair and put it in a high ponytail. A little spray and a couple of bobby pins to get rid of the flyaways, and I was ready for TV. One last check in the mirror, and then I slipped down the back stairs to the dressing rooms.

Chapter 12

I got to the bottom of the stairs and headed toward the back door of 43B. The dressing rooms had front doors that faced the huge hallway of the production facility, and back doors opening onto the stage itself. I gingerly stepped over cables, avoiding props. It was dark, and I could hear someone boo-hooing on one of the sets. I paused to listen. It sounded like Melanie Piven taping a scene. She could cry at the drop of a hat. I was jealous. It usually took me hours of thinking about horrible past events in my life, or devastating fantasies about the future, for me to form tears. If that didn't work, I'd have to put on *Oprah* and hope for the best. I am a method actor, and it can be exhausting, not to mention depressing! Some actors are able to cry if someone just looks at them funny. Life is truly not fair.

I quietly knocked on the door of 43B and put my ear to it, listening for a response. Nothing. Slowly I turned the knob and pushed.

"Hellooo? Anyone in here? Nobody naked, I hope!" I can't tell you how many times I'd been walked in on half dressed.

The room was empty except for a pile of clothes on the floor. Priscilla had clearly finished work and just dropped her wardrobe where she stood. Now, that really pissed me off. Since when was the wardrobe department supposed to be our personal maid service? I always wondered if these slobs were raised in caves. Hang up your own clothes! Okay, deep breaths!

I looked around Barry's room. There was a waiting list for dressing rooms, which meant some actors moved from room to room until a coworker with a permanent room left or got fired. I hadn't been on the show long enough to have my own room, so I was a floater. Barry had been on the show for at least fifteen years and had had this room most of that time. I thought he had decorated it well. Masculine, yet tasteful and not too macho. The walls were a calming shade of taupe with large, framed black-and-white prints on the walls. There was a large mahogany armoire that held a flat-screen TV with several drawers below it. Candles had been placed on the coffee table and sofa tables. The lighting was soft and diffuse.

I picked up Priscilla's clothes and started to put them on hangers. I couldn't help myself; I wasn't perfect by a long shot, but it really bugged me when actors . . . Never mind.

I hung a dress in the closet and noticed something shiny at the back of the shelf, above the rod. Standing on my tiptoes, I reached for it. It was a picture frame holding a photo of Barry, Shana and another couple I had never seen before. A recent photo, from the looks of it. They all had big smiles on their faces, and the picture had been taken at some event. Maybe I was just bitter because of my own (non) relationship with my ex-husband, Randy, but it seemed strange to me. Were they still a couple or not? I was confused.

I put the frame back on the shelf and looked around the room. Something caught my eye. The drawers at the bottom of the armoire had locks. Not unusual. Sometimes actors kept personal items at work, and they didn't want someone ripping them off. I tried opening the top drawer. Locked. I took a bobby pin out of my hair and stuck it in. After a second of jimmying, it opened. I was getting good at this! Or it was a cheap lock.

I slid open the drawer. There were only hygiene products: mouthwash, lotion, shower gel. I tried the next drawer down. It was locked, too, but I picked it. I couldn't believe it! It looked like a pharmacy in there. Prescription bottles of all shapes and sizes. They all seemed to be painkillers and anti-inflammatories. Wow, Barry must have severe back pain or a severe drug problem. I examined a couple of bottles. Some had Barry's name on the label, and some had Shana's. Medication with her name on it and a recent photo in his closet? I wasn't just bitter. This was definitely odd. I picked up a few more bottles and noticed the same doctor, Eugene Reynolds, had prescribed them all.

Just then, I heard the front door open. I quickly

closed the drawer, but my hands were still holding four bottles! I put them behind my back.

"Who's there?" I asked.

"Hey, Alex, what are you doing in here? This isn't your room today." Jennifer from wardrobe poked her head around the corner. "You're in 43C."

"Oh, really? Thanks. I guess I read the room run-down wrong!" I tried covering my surprise. "I'll just head over next door."

"I'm picking up Priscilla's clothes. Oh, my God! It's a miracle! They're hung up!" She squinted and looked at me. "Did you do this?"

"I might have, yeah. No biggie."

"Thanks. Hey, really shocking about Shana Stern, huh? Barry must be devastated; they were so close." Jennifer was moving toward the sofa, and I was afraid she was settling in for a long conversation. Just then, a loud voice came booming over the speaker on the wall.

"Moving to item thirteen: Brad, you have a one-scene standby, and Alex, you have a two-scene standby. Moving to item thirteen . . ." I was saved by Herbie, our stage manager.

"Yikes! I gotta go get dressed. We'll catch up later, Jen," I backed out of the room, still holding the bottles behind me.

Chapter 13

After stashing the bottles, I quickly changed into my wardrobe for the scenes I had coming up. I hadn't even gone over my lines yet. Thank God I didn't have too much to say. The writers had killed off my evil twin, so I wasn't pulling double duty anymore. And I wasn't in the middle of a big story line at the moment. This was good for me as a mom, because I had more time with Sarah, but not so good as the sole breadwinner in my family. I got paid by the episode, after all.

I pulled out my script and looked over the dialogue. Pretty straightforward. I was just about to call Jakes when I was summoned to set. I ran out the back door and gingerly stepped over a multitude of cables to get to my character's living room set. My costar and newest on-screen love interest, Brad Lamont, was waiting for me.

"Let's run this while the cameras move over," he said.

"Good idea," I agreed, and so we did—about ten times, which was nine times too many for me. I feel that running lines too much makes them stale, but a lot of other actors like to do it. It proved to be a good move today, though, because we did all our scenes in one take each.

I was leaving the set to go call Jakes when a bunch of the crew came over to ask me about Shana.

"What happened, Alex? Do the cops have any leads?" Mikey, one of the boom operators, asked me.

Cheeks, a camera operator who seemed to have a lot of information, asked, "I heard she had her throat cut in the haunted house at the Playboy Mansion. Is that true?" Word got around fast!

"Yeah, that's true, Cheeks. But I don't know about any leads, Mikey. Sorry. I'll keep you posted, though. I promise." I was desperately trying to keep my professional life and sleuthing life separate. Not easy. But I was happy to see that so many people cared.

I got back to the dressing room and was careful to lock both doors. I pulled the prescription bottles out of a drawer I had hidden them in and scanned the labels. Vicodin, oxycodone, Keflex and vancomycin.

I sat down on my sofa and looked at my scene rundown. I had a good three hours before working again, so I took out my laptop and turned it on. But first I had to call Jakes. I tried his cell, but it clicked over to his voice mail, so I left a message. I was going to call his office, then decided maybe that wasn't such a good idea. Sometimes his buddies and higher-ups were critical of my involvement. Better wait for his call. In the meantime, I could check out what these medications of Barry's and Shana's were used for.

I typed the names into Google and quickly got

the results. The first two were most commonly used as painkillers, and the second two after surgery to combat infection. It was quite obvious that Shana wasn't shy about going under the knife, but Barry? He looked fairly homegrown to me. And who would need so many pills? I knew a little about plastic surgery, but clearly there were all sorts of procedures being done today I didn't know about. But I knew someone who did.

I changed back into my street clothes and checked over my lines to make sure I remembered what I would be doing in the next few scenes. Then I headed out the back door of my dressing room and quietly into 43B. I had to relock those drawers I had jimmied. The only problem was how do you do that once I'd opened them with a bobby pin.

I got down on my knees and saw it was a spring lock. I set the spring and shut the drawer. I pulled, and it held. Hooray!

I looked around to make sure I had covered my tracks, then retraced my steps back into my room and out the front door. As I was walking down the hall to the elevator I pulled out my cell and called Herbie, the stage manager.

"Herbie! I'm going to be out of the building for a little while. Call me if you need me, will ya?" Herbie is a doll and always has my back.

"Sure thing, honey. See you, ummm . . . probably right after lunch." That gave me just about three hours. I could do it. Bel Air Estates was only twenty minutes from the studio. But I'd have to hurry.

Chapter 14

Riley Scott is one of those friends you have who, if nothing else, is entertaining. One whom you never know what they're going to do next—although, with Riley, it usually involved plastic surgery. She had something done after each marriage or live-in relationship ended, which meant she was going to the doctor every two or three years. If anybody could be my expert on plastic surgery, she could.

She had become a fabulously wealthy woman by combining settlements from each husband. After number six, she moved herself to Bel Air Estates. When her maid showed me to the pool, I expected to find her with a fresh bandage covering something.

Riley's real name was Marianne Weber; she was born in a small town in Iowa. She had won a Miss Something or Other back in the day, and came to Hollywood to pursue the Dream. I had met Marianne in an acting class when we were both in our early twenties. She was a very sweet person, and we became friends and stayed friends, even after I started working as an actress and she didn't. Riley was a very pretty girl, but she didn't have much talent and wasn't tall enough to model. As a result, she began reinventing herself. First she changed her name and got boobs and a nose job.

Soon after came husband number one, an Eastern European businessman. And she was off and running. She lived fast and furiously. Although it looked as though her life was glamorous and fabulous, one couldn't help but think it was all so sad.

Each of her surgeries made her more perfect than the one before, and yet she couldn't stop. It wasn't as if she wanted to look like anyone else. She wasn't having Barbie doll surgeries; she was having procedures that made her just look more, well, Riley. An exaggerated version of herself.

Out by the pool, Riley, clad in a string bikini, was lying on a chaise longue. Her surgically enhanced boobs looked as if they were about to burst, with only the smallest strips covering her nipples.

"Mrs. Peterson, ma'am," her maid said.

Riley opened her eyes, looked at me from behind rose-colored sunglasses and smiled.

"Alex! I am so happy to see you, girl. How are you?" She stood up and grabbed a robe from the back of the lounge. "Maria, bring Alex a—"

"Iced tea," I said, quickly.

"Ohhh, good idea! Long Island?" Riley asked.

"I'm working." I looked at Riley apologetically. "Just regular iced tea, thanks," I said to Maria.

"Yes, ma'am."

Riley belted her robe, and then hugged me. Her

body was as solid as marble. The skin of her face was as smooth as a baby's as she pressed her cheek to mine. Her nose was perfect, as were her lips. About the only thing on her that hadn't been worked on—except for some dye—was her hair, which was long, black, and all hers.

"Pull up a chaise and tell me why you're here. It's so wonderful to see you! How's Sarah?" Riley always got a little wistful when she asked about Sarah. She had everything, but had never had children. She said she didn't really want them. Maybe that was true. It felt like regret to me, but what did I know?

"She is just so great. Getting so big. She's in first grade. Loves ballet and she's surfing now . . ." I was starting to gush, so I stopped myself.

"Well, being a mom certainly agrees with you. You look younger than ever, by the way. I don't know how you do it without help." She looked at me closely. "Have you had any help, Alex? Hmmmm?"

"I'm afraid of knives and needles."

"My two best friends," she said, and laughed.

"I'm not quite sure where to start," I said, honestly. "I need to talk to an expert."

"Regarding what?"

"Plastic surgery."

"You want the name of my doctor?" she asked, raising her lasered eyebrows.

"No," I said, "you're my expert witness."

"Oh," she said, understanding. "You want an expert on the other side of the knife. Well, I think you've found your girl."

I often wondered why an intelligent woman felt the need to subject herself to so many surgeries. Riley was smart and she knew it, but she was also insecure. She knew that, too. Weren't the constant procedures supposed to take care of that? I doubt that they did. The day one of the surgeries improved her self-esteem, I suspect it would be her last.

The maid returned with my iced tea, which I accepted with thanks.

"That'll be all, Maria."

"Yes, ma'am."

I sipped my tea and set the glass on the small table next to me.

"What's going on, Alex?" she asked.

"Shana Stern was killed two days ago," I said.

"I know. I read about it in the paper." She hugged herself.

"She invited me to that party. There was something she wanted to tell me. Unfortunately, she never got the chance."

"That's very sad. I still don't know what I can do, though."

"It's a long story, but I found these pills with Shana's name on them." I took the prescription bottles from my purse and passed them to her.

"I have these in *my* medicine cabinet," she said.

"For after your surgeries?" I asked.

She nodded.

"Basically, they help with the pain." She looked at me. "I say *help with* because nothing really works completely."

She handed them back.

"So you think Shana had plastic surgery? She was a *Playboy* Playmate; that wouldn't be unusual, would it?"

"I know. I was just wondering," I said. "What about procedures people don't hear so much about? I know doctors in Los Angeles and New York, even Mexico, are doing things that mainstream America doesn't know about."

"Hmmm. I'll have to think about that. What have I had done?" She looked at herself as if she were looking at a piece of real estate. "My calves have implants; my butt and chin and cheeks, and breasts, of course. I've had lots of lipo. Collagen for my lips; my nose has been done a couple times. But that's old news. No matter what you do, there always seems to be more you should do, especially as fifty is rearing its very ugly head! The one thing they haven't come up with is a way to reverse the aging process. And if they ever do, sign me up!"

"Yeah, I know what you mean." The big five-O was on my radar, too. "What about plastic surgery for men? Are they doing anything new these days?"

I wondered whether maybe Barry had been a patient of this Dr. Reynolds, too. But I didn't see any reason to mention his name at this point.

"Well, yes, of course! But men are so much more discreet about it. Or embarrassed. You know . . . the standards. Calves, chins, love handles, lipo. They can even create a six-pack by doing a procedure called etching on their stomachs. It's endless. Why are you interested in men's surgeries if you're asking about Shana?" She looked at me with one raised eyebrow.

"I'm just grasping at straws. It's frustrating knowing that she had something to tell me and was killed before she could. I can't help thinking she was reaching out to me for help." I passed one of the bottles back to her. "What about the doctor's name? Does it ring a bell?"

"Eugene Reynolds," she said, shaking her head. "No. I've used a half dozen doctors in the LA area. That name isn't familiar." She handed the bottle back. "I have all my work done here in LA. He could be from Orange County or wherever."

I put the bottle back in my purse, then took another sip of iced tea.

"Do you think these medications are connected to her murder?" Riley asked.

"I don't know," I said, "but I wanted to check with you to see if you knew the doctor, or if you could confirm what I was thinking about the pills."

"Well, I've used all of them after some of my surgeries," Riley said.

I checked my watch. It was close to noon, and God forbid I was late for my scenes.

"I won't bother you any more with this, Riley," I said, standing up. "Thanks."

"You're not bothering me! It's fun to talk to you about my 'hobby.' Are you sure you have to go?" she asked, also standing. "I mean, I have the afternoon free. . . ."

"I have to get back to work, or I'd stay," I said. "But I can come back sometime and we'll catch up."

"Please," she said, "do that. And bring Sarah!"

I had the feeling she was lonely and wanted some company. I guessed that she didn't have a man in her life at the moment—which wasn't surprising, because men didn't last very long in her life.

Maria appeared at that moment, and Riley said, "Maria, will you show Alex out, please?"

"Yes, ma'am."

"I'll talk to you soon, Alex," Riley said.

"Thanks again, Riley."

As I followed Maria back into the house, I could see Riley take off her robe and recline on the chaise. She looked perfect.

Chapter 15

I jumped in the car and checked my cell. There were two voice mails.

"Hey, baby, I got your message. I was in a meeting. Call me back." Jakes had returned my call.

The second one was from Herbie. "Alex, get your butt back here! We're moving very fast and could get to you by twelve thirty!" *Click.* Oh, shit! I looked at the clock. Twelve fifteen. My worst nightmare: keeping everyone on set waiting for me.

I threw the cell in my purse and hauled ass down Sunset Boulevard back to Highland, rushing to get to the studio as fast as I could. I pulled into the studio parking lot at exactly twelve thirty. As I ran into my dressing room, someone was knocking on the back door.

"Alex! Are you in there? We've been looking for you!" It was Herbie. He didn't sound at all happy.

I yelled back. "Yeah, Herb, I'm here. Just having some, umm . . . woman problems." I hated going there, but a girl's got to do what a girl's got to do. I threw on my wardrobe, slapped on some lip gloss, took a deep breath and opened the back door.

"Sorry, Herbie. What can I say?"

He just looked at me and said, "Go!"

So I went.

I had managed to get there just in time, thank you very much, and the rest of the taping went along smoothly.

Later, back in my dressing room, I returned Jakes's call.

"Where you been? I've been waiting to hear from you!"

I answered after a sigh, "Busy day. And I have lots to tell you. Why don't you come over for dinner tonight?" I didn't want to fill him in on everything over the phone.

"What about Sarah? You think she's ready to—"

I stopped him. "She's going to a friend's for dinner. And my mom has plans. I'll see you tonight. Anything special you want?"

"Surprise me."

"You got it."

I changed my clothes and headed out the door. Once in the elevator I had to lean against the back wall. What a day! Manipulating a makeup artist for info, almost getting busted in Barry's room and two seconds from being late for work. That was enough excitement to last me a while.

*   *   *

I got back in my car and headed south on the Santa Monica Freeway. I couldn't help thinking I should get a new car. I was weird about my vehicles. They sort of became family members to me and I had a hard time parting with them. But this was getting silly.

I was driving what I called my kid car, a 1999 Ford Explorer. The car had been in an accident not long ago, but it hadn't been totaled. The insurance company had footed the bill, and the car had been repaired. Still, it didn't drive the same or feel the same. And we still didn't know who had run me off the road, although Jakes suspected it might be my ex, Randy. I didn't want to believe that the father of my daughter would try to hurt me like that, but . . .

I drove to Venice and stopped at a small grocery store. It was a throwback to those neighborhood stores that were quickly becoming corporations. It made me feel like I was part of a community. I liked that. I called home to check on Sarah.

"Sarah's already at her play date. And I'm going out with Marjorie for dinner."

I was happy Mom had made some friends and was actually getting a life of her own. Sarah was doing well in school and had some good friends. I had a great job, not as great as others I'd had, but a job nonetheless, and a relationship I was excited about. Things were looking good.

I smiled to myself as I walked the aisles of the grocery store. I found myself in the frozen food section first. Pistachio ice cream. Sarah's favorite. I tossed that into the cart. I was still trying to make up my mind about dinner when I suddenly noticed someone standing in front of me. I stopped short.

"Hello, Alex."

It was Randy.

Chapter 16

I had several urges.

The first was to punch him in his still-handsome face.

The second was to run.

The third was just to scream.

I did none of those things.

He picked up the ice-cream carton from the shopping cart. "Pistachio," he said. "Still my little girl's favorite?"

"You son of a bitch," I said, finding my voice.

"Take it easy, Alex." He put the ice cream back. "I'm just here to talk."

"How did you find me?"

"I followed you from work."

"Get away from me, Randy," I said.

"What the hell is wrong with you?" he demanded. "I just want to talk."

Randy had a way of convincing himself he was the wounded party. How he could muster that kind of indignation, I never knew. It was false to everyone but him.

"I don't want you near me."

"Hey," he said, "the last time we saw each other, *you* punched *me* in the face."

"You tried to kill me, you son of a bitch!"

"What are you talking about?"

"I'm talking about the night you chased me on PCH and drove me off the road."

"I don't know what you're talkin' about," he said. "Look, I've been tryin' to get my life together, tryin' to find a job, stayin' away from you and Sarah until I was settled. Now I am, and I want to talk about custody."

"Custody? Are you crazy, Randy? After you tried to kill me?"

"I just told you, I didn't try to kill you!"

Suddenly, I realized everyone in the store was looking at us. I left the shopping cart where it was and headed for the door.

Outside, Randy came up from behind and grabbed my arm. I yanked it away and turned on him.

"If you touch me, I'll start screaming."

He backed off, putting his hands up.

"Look," he said, "obviously this is a bad time."

"Are you trying to be funny?" I asked. "Or are you just stupid?"

"Look, Alex," Randy said, "take it easy. I'm just tryin' to get back into my little girl's life—"

"That's not going to happen, Randy," I said, cutting him off. "You're not getting back into her life or mine."

"Don't flatter yourself," he snapped. "I don't want

you; only her. I'm filing for joint custody. I already have a lawyer, and he says I have a good shot."

"What kind of a lawyer would tell you that?" I asked. "Didn't you tell him that you stole my money, left us with nothing?"

"I didn't steal—"

"You stole money from me and from your clients," I said. "You should be in jail."

"I haven't been convicted of anything, Alex," he said. "And I didn't steal money from you. That was our joint account."

"Did you have joint accounts with all your clients, too?"

"They were covered by insurance," he said. "They all got their money back. Nobody pressed charges."

"Really? We'll just see about that," I said.

"You can't do anything to hurt me, Alex," he said. "I'm filing for joint custody. You can make it easy or you can make it hard, but it's gonna happen."

"Over my dead body."

For a moment, I thought he was going to hit me, and just as quickly I thought he was going to cry.

"Why are you doin' this to me, Alex?"

"W-why am I . . . doing this . . . to you?" I stammered. I was so flabbergasted, I couldn't speak clearly. "My God, Randy . . . you tried to kill me."

"That again?" he snapped. "Stop sayin' that. I did no such thing!"

I backed away from his anger, which seemed so genuine, I was stunned.

"I've had enough," he said, pointing his finger

at me. "I just wanted to tell you what I was doin'. You'll hear from my lawyer."

He turned and stormed away. What right did he have to storm anywhere? I watched him get into a new convertible and drive away. A new car? How the hell did he get a new car?

Surely, there had to be some legal way for me to stop him.

I turned to go back to my car when I remembered why I was there. I went back inside and found my shopping cart untouched. I exchanged the ice cream for a container fresh from the freezer, and then went to the checkout line. I did my best to ignore the looks I was getting from everyone.

Chapter 17

I got home from the store with nothing other than pistachio ice cream to serve for dinner. I looked in the cabinets, but was so flustered that I couldn't think straight. I actually liked to cook—it was sort of a creative outlet for me—but I needed to be somewhat focused. And I definitely wasn't. So I decided to call a restaurant on the corner that delivered.

I didn't know the number, so I dialed 411. But I screwed up. When I heard the lady say "911. What is your emergency?" I remembered what Freud said about mistakes. You know that there really aren't any. And I realized I was in trouble. Apologizing profusely, I hung up.

Dinner was going to have to wait. I grabbed an open bottle of red wine and a coffee cup and walked out the back French doors to the dock. The best thing about my home was that it opened up onto a Venice Beach canal. I sat down and just let myself cry as I watched the ducks float by. I'm not sure how long I was out there, but Jakes came crashing out the back door, clearly upset.

"What are you doing? I was shouting your name. I thought something happened to you." He looked at me, and seeing I was not okay, asked, "What is it? Is Sarah okay?"

I pulled him down next to me and shook my head. "Sarah's fine. Just hold me." He said nothing, but held my head against his chest and stroked my hair. Not pushing or pressuring me, just letting the lapping of the water on the dock calm me down.

I finally looked at him, and his eyes were so sweet, so open. I smoothed the hair at the nape of his neck and kissed him. He tasted like peppermint. It quickly began to build into something else, and before we knew it, he was gently lifting my shirt over my head. I fumbled with his pants zipper. We made love in a gentle yet frenetic way, right there on the wooden dock in broad daylight. It was as if it was our first time, and in many ways it was. I had never been so available to him, maybe because I felt so vulnerable. He brushed the tears from my cheeks and kissed my eyes and mouth.

"What happened?" he whispered.

I replied simply, "Randy happened."

"What? Randy? That asshole—did he hurt you?"

"No," I said, "not physically. He wants shared custody. I can't deal with that. I can't!" I grabbed my clothes and walked into the house. I was putting on my jeans when he came up behind me.

"It's going to be okay, Alex. One way or another. We'll get through this." He grabbed my shoulders and turned me around. "I'm here. You're not alone in this." He made a point of looking at me. He meant it, and I got it. I wasn't alone in this. And I wasn't sure how I felt about that. Damn. I was really messed up. Like a Gloria Steinem experiment gone horribly wrong. I was so sick of myself. I mean, really sick of myself.

Okay. So I'd been hurt in my life. Who hadn't been? Who? So I shut the fuck up and just said, "Thank you." It took a second, but I managed to squeeze out a timid but sincere, "I need you." I thought he was going to fall over, but he had great composure and just shrugged.

"I mean it," he said. "Now tell me what happened."

"I'm hungry. I didn't get groceries," I said as I looked around the bare kitchen. "Are you okay with Cheerios and bananas?" He nodded, and we grabbed the cereal and milk while I filled him in on Randy.

"Interesting perspective your ex has, Alex. I'm not sure if he's a hundred percent correct in his assumptions, but we'll find out." His whole demeanor made me feel better. I guess it wasn't the end of the world. We'd figure it out, right?

We moved to the living room, spreading our dinner out on the coffee table.

"As if my day wasn't full enough . . ." And I told him about what I had discovered in Barry's dressing room.

"You actually broke into his drawers? You're very gutsy, Alex. That's against the law."

"It was worth it. Look." I retrieved the prescription bottles from my purse and put them on the coffee table in front of us.

"Do you know what this stuff is?" he asked, lifting the bottles to read the labels.

"Yeah. I have people, too. And she confirmed they're used primarily after surgeries, to prevent pain, infection and swelling. The bottles were both in Shana's name and Barry's."

"Barry Stern has already been questioned by phone. He has an alibi for the night of the murder, but I still need to speak to him in person. I need to look into his eyes as he answers questions."

"I found out he's not scheduled to work for a couple of weeks. He's probably at his Vegas home."

"And this doctor? Have you looked him up in the phone book?" he asked.

"No," I said. "But my consultant is positive he's not local."

"Consultant? Look at you." His eyes twinkled as he grinned at me.

"I take this seriously." I jabbed him in the arm.

"Okay, well, let's get a phone book and make sure of that."

I got the yellow pages. We looked through the general MDs, even though I was pretty certain he was a plastic surgeon. Then went on to other specialties.

"Nothing," Jakes said. He picked up the bottles again. "Local pharmacy, but maybe not a local doctor. Some pharmacies are open twenty-four hours. Let's see."

He dialed, got a message telling him the hours of the pharmacy.

"I'll have to check with them tomorrow," he said, breaking the connection.

"But where else do we look now?"

He thought a moment, and then looked at me. We both said, "Google."

Chapter 18

We took out my laptop, put it on the coffee table and sat on the sofa with our knees touching. We got online, went to Google and waited.

"There's got to be a database of doctors," he said. "All we've got to do is find it and put his name in."

I typed in *doctor data base*. Google corrected me and asked if I meant *doctor database*. I clicked on the correction and we got quite a few AMA listings. I just clicked on the first one and was immediately directed to something called Doctorseeker Usage Verification. Underneath it were some squiggly letters and numbers in a box.

"What's that?" Jakes asked.

"Kind of a code," I said. "They want us to copy it over, and if it's right, they'll let us in."

"Why? If this service is available, why make it harder for people?"

"I don't know," I said. "I understand computers just enough to know I have to type these letters into this box." Which I did, then clicked on the SUBMIT button.

The screen blinked and reappeared with this message in red—*Error: The characters did not match the image. Please try again!*

"What did you do?" Jakes asked, annoyed.

"I don't know," I said, just as annoyed. "I put the numbers in right, but it's telling me I didn't."

"Now what?"

"They want me to try again with these numbers."

"Well, make sure you type them in right this time."

"I typed them in right last time."

"Just be careful," he said.

I carefully typed the numbers in.

"See them?" I asked.

"Yeah, they're right."

I hit SUBMIT. We were directed to the Doctorseeker page.

"Looks like a lot of ads," Jakes said.

"Yes, but here it says SEARCH," I said, pointing to the top right-hand corner. "All we have to do is type in the doctor's name and click on GO." I put the cursor on GO and right-clicked my mouse.

Eugene Reynolds generated 179 matches.

"That many?" Jakes said.

"Yes. But see, it says fifty-four percent match, fifty-three percent match. These here are results for gene-splicing experiments, gene patenting, and gene therapy. It's only these seven top matches we have to be concerned with."

"Oh, okay. Seven's not too bad." He leaned forward. "I don't see any addresses."

"Don't you use computers at work?" I asked him.

"Yes, and I have people who run them for me."

"So now I'm your people?"

He leaned over and kissed me. "You better be."

"Move over," I said. "We just have to click on the names."

I put the cursor on the first *Eugene Reynolds* and the name turned red. I clicked.

"Wait, wait," Jakes said, taking out his notebook. We clicked on all seven doctors, and he wrote down each addresses.

"We got Chicago, San Francisco and Nashville," he said. "Boston, Las Vegas, Seattle and . . ." I grabbed his arm.

"Wait! Las Vegas? Barry has a home there. And Barry's name is on some of the bottles! That has to be it!"

"Las Vegas, huh?" He flipped through his notebook.

I looked at the kitchen clock.

"I have to pick up Sarah. . . ."

"'Nuff said." He got up. "Remember, I have people. In fact, one of those people is waiting for me now."

"What's her name?" I asked, trying to be funny.

"Len. We've got some work to do. And, by the way, you did well today! I'm impressed."

"You're pretty impressive, too. In so many ways." I pulled him toward me. "Thanks again."

"I meant what I said. It will be okay. I'll make sure of it." He kissed me, and I teared up.

I had my very own knight in shining armor! And he had a nice butt, too. We both headed out the door and into our respective vehicles.

"I'll call you later!" he yelled over to me.

I blew him a kiss. Corny, but I was feeling it. We drove off in opposite directions.

Sarah and my mom were both safely tucked in. But I couldn't sleep, so a few hours after I went to bed, I got up, made a cup of tea and carried it into the living room. The laptop was still on the coffee table, so I got on the Web. I did a search for Dr. Eugene Reynolds in Las Vegas, Nevada, and found his Web site. There are two kinds of plastic surgery: aesthetic and reconstructive. His specialty, aesthetic, comprised plastic and cosmetic surgery. That meant noses and breasts, butts, lipo. Since we were dealing with a former Playmate and an actor, that seemed logical.

I seemed to have gone as far as I could, so I turned off the computer, finished my tea, put the cup in the sink and went back to bed.

After thinking of all the ways Randy should die, and then feeling guilty for my not-so-enlightened fantasies, I finally drifted off into a fitful sleep.

Chapter 19

I woke up early, ready to take on anything that came my way. Since I had done scenes from three different episodes yesterday, I was off work for a whole week. I made Sarah breakfast and took her to school. I promised I'd be the one picking her up later.

As she ran into school with the other kids, I told my Bluetooth, "Jakes!" Amazingly, it got it right the first time.

"Jakes," he said.

"Did you check with the pharmacy yet?"

"Not yet," he said. "I haven't had time."

"What about the gift basket the stalker gave Shana? Any news?"

"Not yet. They're still processing it. Slow down. These things take time."

"Sorry. I guess I'm feeling kind of antsy. I found out last night that Dr. Reynolds is an aesthetic plastic surgeon—you know boobs, nose jobs, et cetera. He's got to be the one."

"I'll check with the pharmacist and let you know what happens."

"But what do I do now?" Silence. "Oh, c'mon! Jakes! Sarah's at school; I'm not working. Give me something to do!"

He took pity on me and agreed to meet for lunch.

Jakes was waiting at a table when I arrived. I have to say one thing about him: He rarely, if ever, keeps me waiting. Nine times out of ten he's the first to arrive, which I appreciate. There's nothing worse than having a waiter or waitress try to entertain you while you sit and wait.

He stood up as I approached the table and kissed me quickly on the mouth.

"How was your morning?" he asked as I sat.

"Uneventful," I said. "What did you find out from the pharmacy?"

"Just what you thought," he said. "The doctor who prescribed the medicine is your guy. He called the prescriptions in for Shana."

"So she went to him for plastic surgery. For what—new breasts?"

"That we don't know," he said. "I have to go and see the ME later today. Hopefully, he'll have more information for us."

"Us?"

He smiled and said, "Len and me."

"Oh."

"Don't tell me you want to go to the morgue with me, Alex!" he said. "You don't want to see Shana that way, do you?"

"No." Did I? Maybe a teensy-weensy bit. But I decided against that sensorial nightmare, and said, "I don't. But I'll be interested in what you find out."

"And I'll tell you," he said. "Now let's order, huh?"

Over dessert, Jakes asked, "What's wrong? You look low."

"I'm just feeling . . ."

"What?"

"Well, I spent last night on the computer and yesterday with Riley trying to find out what you got by talking to a pharmacist."

"So?"

"So I wasted my time."

"What else would you have done with that time?"

I hesitated, then said, "I don't know."

"Why'd you do the computer research last night?"

"I couldn't sleep."

"So that means you found out about the doctor before I did."

"Yeah, but you got it confirmed by a licensed pharmacist."

"I'm a cop, remember. And this is not a competition, Alex," he said. "We both got the same information in a different way. That's all."

"Well, I wasted my time with Riley."

"Why?"

"She couldn't tell me who the doctor was, or any-

thing about the medication I didn't already know—
or you didn't get from the pharmacist. It was a
waste."

"I wouldn't worry about it," he said. "Finish your
cake."

After we left the restaurant, we walked arm in arm
to my car.

"Hey, how's it going with your new boss?" I
asked.

Jakes used to have a female captain he said had
a thing for him. When he turned her down, she
started giving him hell. She had also never liked me.
But she had been replaced a month ago by a man
named Campbell.

"Campbell's okay," he said. "I worked with him before, a long time ago when we were both detectives."

"And now he's a captain."

"I know," he said. "And I'm still a detective. I like
being a detective."

"So you've told me."

One of the many things I'd learned about Jakes
was that he didn't like bosses and didn't want to be
a boss. I understood that this was a choice on his
part, not a lack of ambition.

"So, what will you do now?" I asked.

"Talk to the ME; try to get that Vegas doctor on
the phone. What are you going to do with the rest of
your day?" he asked.

"Some shopping, pick up Sarah from school, make
dinner . . . you know, mom and housewife stuff."

"You're no housewife."

"I was."

"Miss it?"

"No," I said, "Because I was married to that bastard—" I stopped short.

"You want to talk about Randy?" he asked.

"No."

"Want me to go find him and throw him a beating?"

"Yes," I said. Then, "No."

I leaned into him.

"I just can't believe he would sue for custody and be taken seriously by any court."

"As far as I can tell, he hasn't been convicted of anything."

I shook my head. "This is crazy."

"Why don't you wait and see whether he really does it?" Jakes said. "Then we can decide what to do."

"We?" I asked.

"Yes," he said, "we."

Chapter 20

I did some shopping for incidentals—lipstick, eye shadow, mascara; the kind of shopping a woman can do on automatic pilot—all the while thinking of Shana and plastic surgery. I was wishing she had some family or friends I could talk to, but that didn't seem to be the case. And if she'd had someone to confide in, why would she have come to me?

I had studied the dates on the prescription bottles several times. We knew the dates of the three were the same, but I couldn't remember what it was.

While I sat parked in front of Sarah's school, waiting for her to be dismissed, I took out the bottles and checked them again. They were all from last year. I took out my cell phone and called Jakes.

"Miss me already?" he asked.

"Yes," I said, "but I also have a question."

"What is it?"

"Did you ask the pharmacist when Shana first filled her prescriptions?"

"Yeah, I did. Hold on." I knew he was taking out his notebook. I kept my eyes on the front door of the school. I recognized some of the children coming out, so I knew Sarah was on her way. I opened the car door, preparing to get out.

"Here," he said, and read me the dates. They were the same as the dates on the bottles in my hands.

"These bottles have that same date, and they're not empty," I said. "Looks like she never renewed the prescriptions."

"She never used them up?" he said. "Maybe she didn't need them."

"She didn't strike me as someone who had a high pain threshold," I said.

"Maybe she was a quick healer."

"What did the ME have to say?" I asked.

I could hear paper, like he was opening the ME's report.

"He found scars on her breasts," he said. "You know, consistent with incisions for breast implants."

"Not a surprise."

"And he found saline implants, size thirty-eight double-D."

"Ouch."

"Okay, but here's a surprise," he said. "He found something odd about the skin around her eyes."

"What do you mean, *odd*?"

"He said the flesh around her eyes was kind of thin," Jakes explained.

"What does that mean?"

More pages moving. "I don't know. That's all it says. I'll check with him."

"Okay, so what's next? Did you talk to the doctor in Las Vegas?"

"That's a problem," Jakes said. "Nobody's answering his office phone. We're trying to find another listing for him, home or cell. We also had Las Vegas PD send a car to his house, but nobody was there."

"Did they go inside?"

"They refused," Jakes said. "There's no probable cause to break into his house."

"Really? Shana's been murdered! That's not probable cause?"

"There's no proof the doctor is involved. And the murder took place here, not in their jurisdiction."

"So," I surmised, "it sounds like we need to go to Vegas."

"We?" he asked.

"That's right, we. I was asked to go there this weekend for a soap opera fan event called Daytime in the Desert. I didn't want to go because I had too much on my plate, but it sounds like it could work out perfectly. Then you can talk to Barry."

"A little work; a little play. I like it. We haven't gotten away together yet. So. Just you and me in Sin City, huh?" Jakes actually sounded kind of excited, in a Jakes-understated sort of way.

"Yeah, just you and me." I was getting excited, too. Maybe we could see a show, be alone for a couple of days and see how we were together away from home. I'd still be working, but not so much at night.

"I'll have Sarah and my mom stay with George and Wayne, you know, just in case Randy tries something stupid. It's probably not necessary, but it would make me feel better."

Jakes was saying something, but I was only half listening. Sarah hadn't come out yet. I looked at the clock on the dash. She was a little later than usual. Not by that much, but she definitely was. Then a slow panic began to creep up. Where was she? Had Randy gotten her? Would the school let her go with him? I must have let out a gasp, because Jakes's voice snapped me back to the moment.

"What's wrong, Alex? Are you okay?" he asked.

"Sarah isn't out yet. She's always out by now. Oh, my God. What if—" Just then, Sarah came running out, struggling to put on her backpack.

"Oh, thank God. She's here." My whole body flooded with relief. "Sorry about that. Can I call you right back?" I hung up after he said yes, and jumped out of the car. Sarah saw me, waved and started running toward me. I picked her up and hugged her tightly.

"Mommy, ow! Too tight!" she said pushing me away.

"I'm sorry, sweetheart. I just missed you so, so much today." I put her down and kissed her head all over. "I love you."

"I love you, too, Mommy. Can we stop at Starbucks and get a Strawberries and Crème?"

"Sure we can. Let's go!" I grabbed her hand and we jumped in the car. I was wiping tears of relief off my face as we drove away. Then I realized. There was no way I was going to Vegas without Sarah. Who was I kidding?

But how was I going to parent my child, be a sexy, fun-loving girlfriend, entertain the fans, investigate a murder and avoid my mother's disapproval all at the same time?

Chapter 21

"We're going to Las Vegas, Nevada? All of us?"

"I'm going to Daytime in the Desert—a big event for soap opera fans. It'll be fun! Vegas is a family town, now, too. There are lots of kid-friendly things to do. And the food! Great food. Mandalay Bay even has a beach. With real waves!"

Was I pouring it on a little too thick? Maybe. But Mom was giving me that look. Skepticism oozed from her pores.

"What?"

"I thought you hated those things."

"I hate the structure, but I love fans. Where would I be without them? They actually care about the show and the characters. And I do enjoy giving back in a more personal way. I mean it. But also . . . the show wants me to go. Okay? They want me to go. And I want to be a team player. It doesn't hurt to keep the powers that be happy, right?"

"Why do I get the feeling you're not telling me everything?" My very wise and very annoying mother asked me pointedly.

"I don't know what you mean." And then to distract her, I added, "You have to pack. Go. Go. We're leaving in the morning. Bring a swimsuit. Go."

She stared at me, glaring in a way that used to make me confess everything when I was a teenager. I was pleased that it didn't work anymore. I stared right back at her, and eventually she relented and walked out the back door toward the guesthouse, presumably to pack.

One down. Now I had to tell Jakes that there was a small glitch with our romantic getaway weekend. I called him on his cell.

"Hey, babe. Are you getting ready? What time should I pick you up in the a.m.?" This was going to be more difficult than I had thought. He sounded really excited. How very cute!

"Jakes, slight problem. I, uh, I just don't feel a hundred percent good about leaving Sarah in LA, even with George. Randy is a loose cannon. You know? I mean, he probably wouldn't try anything, but you never know with him. I'd be worried the whole time." I felt bad. Really bad. "Sorry." I kind of muttered.

Jakes didn't miss a beat.

"No problem. So, what? You want to bring her along? How does that work?"

"Well." I took a breath. "My mom and Sarah and I will fly in to Vegas. A limo will pick us up and be at our disposal the whole time. This operation is pretty first-class, apparently; they're even putting me up at the Bellagio in a nice, big fat suite. Can you get a room there, too? Then even if we can't be alone all the time, we'd still be close."

"You're funny," he said. "I'll be lucky if the department gives me enough cash for a Motel 6. But it's okay! This can still work out. I'm gonna drive there; I like the drive through the desert. I would have preferred to make it with you, but that's cool. It gives me time to think and work out some questions about Shana's murder. We'll hook up in Vegas and take it from there." He sounded all right, but I wasn't completely sure.

"You really okay with this? I gotta do what I gotta do, you know what I mean? She's my kid. . . ."

"Of course I'm okay. You wouldn't be the woman you are if you didn't take care of Sarah the way you do. And the woman you are is the woman I'm crazy about. It's all good." It was better than good. He was awesome. And I was tearing up.

We said we'd touch base once in Vegas. I still had my phone in my hand after hanging up. I couldn't quite let it go, because something was bugging me. He had said he was fine with Sarah and my mom coming along, and I believed him, but something was different. I couldn't put my finger on it. Maybe I was just being insecure.

I shook it off, because now I had some packing to do. Viva Las Vegas!

Chapter 22

"Mommy! This is fun!" My darling daughter was standing on the limo seat with her head sticking up through the sunroof, the hot desert wind whipping her blond hair all over her face. The driver was not amused. He kept looking disapprovingly in his rearview mirror.

"Sarah, get down from there. That's enough!" I looked at the driver and gave him a kids—what-are-you-gonna-do-with-'em? look. He just shook his head. That kind of pissed me off. So I got up on the seat and stuck my head up through the sunroof, too. Sarah was right. It was fun.

We were zipping down Las Vegas Boulevard—the Strip—and even at one in the afternoon, the town was hopping. Streets were filled with a multitude of tourists in Bermuda shorts on their way to shop, eat and, of course, gamble. We waved at them as we sped past the MGM Grand, New York–New York, Monte Carlo, and Planet Hollywood, and they waved back. Even the crazy-hot air was exhilarating in a strange way.

"Alexis! Get down from there. What are you doing? That's not a good example for Sarah." Apparently, it was my mother's turn to try to control the situation. I heard the limo driver saying something I couldn't quite make out, and then suddenly there was Mom! Right next to Sarah and me.

"That driver has some nerve. He said some very rude things about your parenting, and threatened to take us back to the airport. I'll show him some good parenting. Ahhh! My hair." I watched her newly permed hair being whipped into a first rate 'fro and laughed.

"What's so funny? You think you're looking your best right now? It looks like you put your finger in a light socket," she yelled, and started laughing.

Pretty soon all three of us were holding on to each other and cracking up. We must have looked a sight. Three generations of crazy Peterson women soaking up the Vegas vibe.

I got back inside the car and quickly placated the driver. Within a few minutes, we had pulled up in front of the Bellagio, right across from the faux Eiffel Tower of the Paris.

"Miss Peterson! Miss Peterson! You are so beautiful!" Really? Beautiful? My hair was standing on end and I had desert-induced sweat dripping off my nose. Makeup that had once been applied to my eyelids I was pretty certain was in a puddle at my feet. Only one sort of person could be kind enough to see me as beautiful at that moment. It had to be a fan. I looked around, and sure enough, there was a crowd of people thrusting photos (some of which I would have preferred remain in the archives) and paper and pens at me.

Daytime in the Desert was being held at the Las Vegas Hilton, which was more of a convention hotel than a lot of the others. I had a limo to take me to and fro, and that was nice; in theory, if talent had rooms away from the venue, we could come and go at our hotel without any commotion. In theory. Apparently, word had gotten out that we were staying at the Bellagio. That was okay, I guess. It was just that sometimes fans went a little overboard. Once or twice I'd even been followed into the ladies' room. A woman once reached beneath a stall to hand me a picture and a pen. What could I do? I signed it. After I washed my hands, of course.

I did my best to pose for photos and sign autographs, while slowly making my way toward the entrance.

"Did you just get in, Alex? How was your flight?" a woman of about seventy asked. "You're the first actor to arrive. Are Brad and Priscilla coming in soon? You know, I've been watching from the very first day. *The Bare and the Brazen* is so lucky to have you!"

I was worried about her. It was awfully hot, and I didn't want her to faint.

"Do you need some water or something?" I asked her. She assured me she was fine and held up a bottle of water she was carrying in a tote.

I was handing back a signed photo when somebody in the very rear of the crowd caught my eye. I could see him only from the back, but still he looked vaguely familiar. I tried to get a better look when suddenly I heard a voice from behind me.

"Ms. Peterson? I'm Shelly Watkins. I've been assigned to you this weekend. May I take anything?"

I handed her my large purse. "Yeah, this. Thanks," I answered while I gave a very hot and sweaty fan her very sweaty pen back and posed for a photo with her sister.

"Thanks so much for coming, you guys. I'll see you tomorrow at the brunch!" I yelled, and waved good-bye to everyone, then pushed my way through the revolving doors. The air-conditioning felt amazing.

"Hi. Thanks," I said to Shelly. I caught my breath. "I'm Alexis. Call me Alex, please. I seem to have lost my bags and my daughter."

"Your mother and daughter are both right over here."

I looked ahead of me and there they were, standing dead center, looking up at the famously gorgeous Bellagio ceiling. Beautiful, fragile, translucent, with hand-blown glass flowers by famed artist Dale Chihuly. They were breathtaking.

"Mommy! It's so pretty here. I love this place. Oh. Look at the garden!" She had spotted the atrium at the back of the lobby, with all its beautiful flowers and manicured bushes. I couldn't wait until she saw the chocolate fountain in the candy store.

"Can I go over there in the garden, Mommy?"

"Hold your horses, honey! Let's get settled in our suite and then we'll check everything out," I said, trying to remain somewhat focused within the cacophony of music and slot machines. Such a strange combination. The Bellagio is so pleasing to the eye, yet it assaults the ear. Well, it is a casino. And certainly sounds like one.

"Here are your keys, Ms. Peterson." She handed me two. "And if you all follow me, we can go on over. You're staying in the High Rollers town house. It's right through here."

Chapter 23

Shelly led us to the right of the main lobby, past the lounge where a pianist was already playing Barry Manilow's greatest hits between the slots and the video poker machines. I'd have to get to those later. I love video poker!

We entered a beautifully decorated anteroom where the walls were graced with framed art and sculptures tucked safely away in well-lit alcoves. Two elevators leading up to floors twenty-three and higher were on the right side. Shelly passed those and led us back out another door and down a hallway.

"Where are you taking us? I had no idea this section of the hotel even existed." I felt like I had entered into a secret, rarefied area seen only by the lucky, very loaded, few. Oh, that's right. I had.

"We're almost there. Right through here." Shelly said as she led us through yet another door.

"Wow!" I couldn't believe what I was seeing. Shelly had opened the door, and before us was the most incredible hotel room I had ever seen. More than a room—it was a house.

Sarah immediately ran off and started exploring. My mom and I followed. It was unbelievable. There were four bedrooms, five bathrooms, a living room with a grand piano, a bar and a huge flat-screen TV. The kitchen was a sight to behold, with state-of-the-art appliances and granite countertops. But who would want to cook with twenty-four-hour room service available? Not me! I found Shelly in the foyer by the front door.

"I hope you'll be comfortable here, Ms. Peterson. If you need anything, don't hesitate to call."

"Oh, I think we'll be very happy here. I have to ask you, though. How did we get this place? Not that I'm complaining." I couldn't help myself. I had to know. This was crazy.

"Oh! Well, the manager of the Bellagio is a huge fan of yours. When he heard you would be staying here, he just had to upgrade you." Some upgrade. I hoped the other actors wouldn't be miffed if they found out. Shelly pulled a card out of her pocket. "Don't hesitate to call if you need something, day or night," she said as she opened the door. "Enjoy."

I stood still a moment to take the place in. It was decorated lavishly in gold and burgundy. Plush pillows graced the velvet sofas, intricate oriental carpets complemented the marble floors and lighting from the chandeliers gave the effect of a beautiful Italian drawing room. Gorgeous! Maybe I should rethink my lifestyle choices. As I looked around, I saw a sealed envelope on the table near the fireplace.

Itinerary for Daytime in the Desert was printed across the front. Sarah came running into the room.

"Mommy, can I have the room with the Jacuzzi tub? And the big bed with the steps? Gramma said she'd take me to the garden, and that lady said there's a candy store with a real chocolate fountain. Can I go swimming?" It had taken Sarah all of two minutes to acclimate to this lifestyle. Like mother, like daughter.

"Whoa, slow down. Let me see what my commitments are first. And yes, you can probably have the room with the high bed. This is so cool, isn't it?" I hugged her, then opened up the envelope and pulled out the itinerary.

There was nothing on the itinerary for today. A free day. The next day, Saturday, was a different story. That's when they got their money's worth. The day started with brunch with the fans from nine until noon. The actors had two hours off, and then at two there was a question-and-answer panel, followed by an autograph session that was supposed to end around five. The day continued with cocktails and dinner from seven until nine. Sunday was a short day. Breakfast with the fans, followed by a photo op by the Hilton pool. My plane left at twelve p.m. Not a lot of time left for snooping around Vegas with Jakes. Just then, my cell rang. I looked at the caller ID. Speak of the devil.

"You would not believe this place. It is so awesome. You have to see it." I sounded like Sarah. "It's a High Roller town house, complete with a fireplace, a grand piano . . . just gorgeous. I miss you. Where are you, anyway?"

"I got in a few hours ago. I left LA when it was still dark. I love driving through the desert in the early, early morning. When are we going to see each other?" He was using that husky voice that still made my heart race.

"Let me call you right back." I hung up. "Mom? Mom! Where are you?" I looked down the hallway as she peeked from around the corner of one of the bedrooms.

"Right here, honey. I'll take this room, okay?"

I loved being able to share the perks of my business with my family. It made it that much more fun.

"Of course, Mom. Whatever you want. Hey, could you watch Sarah for a couple of hours? There are some things I need to take care of." I wasn't lying. There really were things I had to take care of. Jakes things.

"Sure. Go do what you need to do."

Why did I feel guilty? How old was I? Never mind. I called Jakes back.

"Let's meet at a place called Olives," he suggested. "Uh, I believe it's on the main floor. I'll be there in fifteen."

"Yeah, I know it. See you in a few!" I was excited to see him. I quickly freshened up, gave kisses and headed out the door.

Chapter 24

Olives is a contemporary restaurant that overlooks the dancing waters on what they called Lake Bellagio. It was too early for dinner, so we managed to get seated right by a window. We could hear Frank Sinatra singing "Luck Be a Lady," while the waters did their thing.

"I never asked," I said, as we were seated. "Do you gamble?"

"No," he said, "I've never had the time to acquire that particular vice."

"But obviously you've been to Vegas before," I said. "Otherwise, how did you know about this place?"

"I have been here before," he said. "Usually for bachelor parties. But someone recommended Olives to me."

"Who?"

"Somebody I met today," he said.

"Oh. At your hotel?"

"No," he said. "A Vegas detective. She's very nice. Helpful."

"Helpful? You mean with the Shana case?"

"Yeah. With that and, uh, other things."

"You're acting kind of weird, Jakes."

"It was a strange day. I got in early and went right to the local police station."

"Jakes," I said, opening my menu, "why don't you just take your time and tell me what you did today?"

"Okay," he said. "Okay. Well, when I first got to town . . ."

Jakes took me through his day step by step. We agreed I wouldn't ask any questions until he was done. . . .

First he had to go to the headquarters of the Las Vegas Metro Police at 400 East Stewart Avenue.

Upon arrival, he was actually able to talk to the sheriff, the highest-ranking person in the department. He explained about Shana's death and how it might be connected to a doctor who lived in Las Vegas. He also told the sheriff that when he had phoned from LA, he had gotten very little cooperation in contacting the doctor.

"I'm sorry to hear that, Detective," the sheriff said. "Tell you what I'll do. I'll assign a detective to you, to assist in your inquiries."

"I appreciate that, Sheriff," Jakes said.

"But you have to understand one thing."

"What's that?"

"You have no authority here," the sheriff said. "All authority lies with my detective."

"I understand."

"I hope you do," the sheriff said. "We've had some of you LA hotshots out here in the past. I know you tend to think of us as hicks, but we're a large metropolitan police department, Detective. We know what we're doing."

"I'm sure you do, Sheriff," Jakes said. "I'll appreciate any cooperation you can give me."

"I'm going to assign Detective Cushing to you. You'll have to go to 750 Sierra Vista. That's our convention center area command. Covers the convention center and the strip, but Detective Cushing can take you anywhere you want to go. Should I have a car take you there?"

"No, that's okay," Jakes said. "I have a car. Thanks." And then he left.

He had the feeling the sheriff was mollifying him, but he decided to wait until he met Detective Cushing before forming an opinion. The problem was that the sheriff was right: Jakes did think of the Las Vegas PD as a bunch of hicks. Their attitude on the phone had done nothing to change his mind. So far, the sheriff was being cooperative, but Jakes wasn't convinced.

When he got to Sierra Vista, he presented himself to a sergeant out front and asked for Detective Cushing.

"Cushing?" the man asked.

"That's right," Jakes said. "You have a Detective Cushing here, don't you?"

"Uh, well, yeah, we do," the sergeant said.

Jakes showed the man his badge and ID and said, "The sheriff sent me over here to see him."

"The sheriff," the sergeant said.

"Yeah," Jakes said, "you can call and ask him."

"Hold on."

The sergeant picked up his phone and dialed three numbers; he wasn't dialing the sheriff.

"Yeah, I got a Detective Jakes from the LAPD down here asking for Detective Cushing. . . . Uh-huh. Yeah, I know, he says the sheriff sent him. . . . He did? Uh-huh, okay. I'll tell him."

He hung up, and said to Jakes, "Have a seat and Detective, uh, Cushing will be right down."

"So he knows I'm here?"

"Um, yeah, Detective Cushing knows you're here. Just have a seat."

There was a row of multicolored plastic seats with metal legs, the kind you see in a lot of government buildings. Jakes picked out an orange one and sat down to wait.

After twenty minutes, he was about to approach the sergeant again when a dark-haired woman wearing an expensively tailored suit and high heels approached him. She was in her thirties, attractive in a stern sort of way—if you liked that type.

"Detective Jakes?"

He stood up.

"That's right. I'm waiting for Detective Cushing. Is there a prob—"

"No problem, sir," she said. "I'm Detective Cushing." She extended her hand. He went to shake it, but she pulled it back. "Can I see your ID?"

Oh, boy, he thought.

He produced his badge and ID and handed them to the lady detective. Jakes was not a chauvinist. He had worked with many women in the LAPD. He was just surprised that no one—not the sheriff or the desk sergeant—had indicated that Detective Cushing was a woman. Probably their idea of being funny.

Detective Cushing gave Jakes his ID back.

"How can I help you, Detective?"

"Is there somewhere we can talk?" he asked. "Your office? Your desk?"

"I have a better idea," she said, "if you don't mind. I'd like to get out of the building."

"Sure."

"Do you have a problem if we take my car?" she asked.

"No, not at all."

"Good."

She led the way out the front door. Jakes took a quick look behind him and saw the sergeant talking with a couple of men in uniform. They were laughing.

At that point, he felt like the butt of the joke—only he didn't know what it was yet.

Chapter 25

"Wait a minute," I said, staring at him across the table. "Back up."

He took a sip of his café au lait. "How far?"

"Back to the part where Detective Cushing is a lady."

"Oh, that far."

"You said she was attractive in kind of a stern way?" I asked.

"Well, yeah, you know," he said, "the way some businesswomen are when they're dressed for work."

"You mean like your ex-captain?"

"Yeah, kind of like her."

"Jakes, are you playing her down a bit?" I asked.

"Why would I do that?"

"Maybe because you think you need to?" I asked. "Maybe you think I would be jealous?"

"Would you?"

"No," I said. "Okay, never mind. This isn't even the important part." Annoyed with myself for having brought it up, I took a bite of triple-layer chocolate cake and said, "Just go ahead with your story."

"Okay . . ."

Detective Cushing drove them in her Toyota Prius to the Venetian, where they valet parked and then walked up to the Grand Canal Shoppes.

"Why here?" he asked.

"I like it here," she said.

There were shops on both sides of the canal. Gondolas floated by.

"Why don't you tell me what you need while we walk?" she suggested.

He told her about Shana's murder and the medicines they found that led them to the doctor in Las Vegas.

"When we called your department to check on the doctor, we didn't get much cooperation."

"Well . . . whenever you LA boys come to town you, uh, usually have an attitude."

"I hope I'm not projecting any attitude now," Jakes said. "I really need your help—detective to detective."

"Actually, we're not," she said.

"So you're not a detective?"

"No, no, I am, but it's a little different in Vegas than in LA. See, here detective is an assignment, not a rank. If tomorrow they wanted to stick me on traffic duty, I'd just be a police officer. Get it?"

"Yes, I do. So what was the joke back at your HQ?"

"What do you mean?"

"They were laughing as we left."

"Yes, well . . . they think I'm a joke there, so they assigned me to Community Relations."

Community Relations was an assignment usually given to someone good with people but not very good with real police work.

"I see." Jakes understood the situation now.

"I can help you, though," she said. "You want to go and check out this doctor?"

"Yeah, I do. Home and office."

"Fine," she said. "Let's do it. Maybe they think I'm a joke back there—the men, I mean—but that doesn't mean I am."

"No, of course not."

"Let me have the doctor's name and his addresses," she said, putting her left hand out. He noticed there was no ring on her finger.

"Would you like a cup of coffee first?" he asked.

"So you noticed she wasn't wearing a ring, and you bought her coffee," I said, finishing up my own cup.

"I'm a detective," he said. "I notice things. And the truth is, I wanted some coffee. It would have been rude not to offer."

"Of course," I said. Jakes suddenly saw something.

"Isn't that your mother and Sarah?"

I nearly dropped my coffee cup. Sure enough, walking by the entrance of Olives were my mom and Sarah. I guess Sarah had gone stir-crazy in the room and needed to explore. They stopped there briefly as Sarah pointed to the fountains in front of the hotel and then continued on their way.

"Let's go say hello."

"No! Jakes, no."

"Why not? Because your mother doesn't know I'm here. Does she?" Jakes looked a little hurt.

"I just wanted to save myself some grief, you know? My mom isn't too thrilled about the whole criminal-investigation thing."

"And not too thrilled with your being involved with me, either. I know."

"It's not personal, Jakes. If she really knew you, I know she'd love you."

"So, what's stopping her from knowing me?" He reached over the table and held my hand. "Alex, I understand your need to protect Sarah. I really do. But I think it's time we came out of the closet, so to speak. I want to know your family." He pulled me closer to him and kissed me softly on the lips.

"Well. That's something we can talk about when we get back to LA, right?"

"No time like the present, Alex." He just stared at me, waiting for an answer. So I gave him the only one I had.

"I can't do this right now. We're in Vegas. I'm working. When we get home, we'll come up with a strategy. Okay?"

"Okay, I'm not going to push. For now." He tossed some bills on top of the check and got up. "Want to come over and check out my fantastic digs? I'll tell you what happened the rest of my day."

We exited the restaurant, making sure the coast was clear of moms, kids and fans, and headed out the rear exit of the hotel to his car.

Chapter 26

We pulled into the parking lot of a motel away from the strip and casinos. I started to open the car door, but Jakes put his hand out and stopped me.

"Give me five minutes. Okay?" Then he pointed. "Room 23, right over there."

"Okay." I was intrigued.

He jumped out and opened the door to his room. I looked around the exterior of the motel, wondering how many hookers had come and gone through those rooms over the course of the past thirty years. Boy, I thought, I bet this place had seen some action. I felt so bad that Jakes was staying here while I was in a palace. And I wondered if I could get him a room at the Bellagio. But would he take it if I could?

I checked my voice mail. Connie had called, of course. I called her back.

"Hey, Al! I'm glad you decided to go." Connie said in her trademark gravelly voice. "Doesn't hurt to stay on the producers' good sides. These days, especially. Be grateful you have a gig. So, how's it goin' in Vegas?"

"It's good, Connie. Pretty typical fan event." I decided what she didn't know wouldn't hurt her.

"Like I said, it's just terrific you went. The town is dead. As a doornail. Nothing's going on with the actors' strike looming. Take the money and run, Al. Take the money and run."

"Sure thing, Connie. Thanks. I gotta go. I'll talk to you next week." I hung up before she could think of something embarrassing I should audition for.

The dash clock said five minutes had passed, so I got out and headed toward the door. It was slightly ajar. When I walked in, I couldn't believe my eyes.

"It's not the Bellagio," he said, "but it's all I've got." He closed the door behind me.

The room was quite dark with the shades drawn and the door closed. Jakes had done an incredible job of changing the ambience of the seedy motel room. On every surface were lit candles. A bottle of champagne was chilling in a plastic ice bucket. Through the open bathroom door I could see a tub, brimming with steam and bubbles. The water was still running.

"Jakes! What are you doing?"

"I wanted Vegas to be romantic. This is the best I could come up with under the circumstances."

"It's amazing. Thank you."

I didn't care where we were at this point. I put my arms around him and hugged him. We kissed slowly and deeply.

"You are so sweet, so sweet," I murmured as he kissed my neck and slowly removed my blouse.

He kissed my breasts lovingly, then undid my skirt. It dropped to the floor. I fumbled with his zipper—jeans and hot weather don't make for easy removal—and tried to slip out of my thong. Finally, we were just skin to skin. I swear that man made me feel like a teenager. But something was different. I pulled away and looked him in the eyes.

"What's going on with you? Are you okay?" I asked.

"I'm better than okay," he said in that sexy, husky voice. He pulled me to him and we made love.

Jakes had always been an amazing lover, but this time there was an intensity about him that really took my breath away. Like he couldn't get enough of me. On top of that, I just hadn't expected him to be so romantic. It both surprised and delighted me.

Before long, we were in the tub, warm, soapy bubbles all around us. It was one of those skinny tubs from the sixties, so I sat inside his spread legs, my back against his chest. We sipped champagne from plastic cups, and he rubbed my neck, worked some kinks out of my back, then slid his hands around to brush against my breasts.

"Hey, hey, tiger," I said, "you never finished telling me about your day." I put my hands over his to stop them from moving. "How about giving me the rest of the story?"

"Not yet," he said. "Let's dry off and get comfortable."

We got out of the bath and started drying each

other with the hotel's threadbare towels. But it didn't matter. It couldn't have been nicer or sexier if we had the fluffiest towels.

Jakes got down on his knees and lovingly dried my legs and thighs. When he was done, he planted a kiss on each knee and stood up. Then he offered me his robe or a dry towel to wrap myself in. I could have wrapped the robe around me twice, so I took the towel.

We left the bathroom and went to the bed.

"Where was I . . . ?" he said, as we lay down and spooned.

Chapter 27

Jakes and Cushing got into her car after they had coffee and she drove to the doctor's office. Jakes knew the address, but he said he wouldn't have been able to find it himself. He and Cushing were talking along the way, comparing notes on their departments and jobs. Actually, he said she was grilling him about working Homicide.

"That's really what I want to do, but it's not going to be easy in this department."

"Are you from here?" he asked.

"Born and bred."

"So it'd be hard for you to leave and try to join some other department?"

"I don't know," she said. "I'd be leaving home. . . ."

"Married?" he asked. "Kids?"

"No husband, no kids. I live alone. Don't even have a cat. Nevertheless, Vegas is home."

"Would you miss the gambling?"

"Gambling's for pros and tourists," she said. "I've never felt the urge."

*   *   *

The doctor's office was in a two-story brick building just on the outskirts of Lake Las Vegas. She parked and they got out, walked up the walk and entered the building. There was a directory in the lobby that led them to the office on the second floor.

"Looks like he has a pretty classy clientele," she said.

"Well," Jakes said, "we know one of them was a *Playboy* centerfold."

"I guess that puts the word *classy* in doubt," she said.

Jakes thought that a bit mean-spirited of Cushing. He wondered whether she'd have said the same thing about a showgirl.

They entered the doctor's office and found themselves in an empty waiting room. Cushing made a show of checking her watch.

"Kind of early to be this empty," she said.

"Maybe his office hours are later today."

There was a woman seated behind a desk out in the open, not behind the typical sliding-glass window. She was in her mid-twenties, makeup expertly applied, just the kind of receptionist you'd expect to find in a plastic surgeon's office. She was wearing a business suit with a skirt. It was obvious the jacket was hiding some impressive—and expensive—assets.

"Doesn't look like there's much business for the doctor today," Jakes said to the girl.

She looked up at them with a bored expression. "Can I help you?"

Jakes looked at Cushing, who took out her badge and showed it to the young woman.

"We're looking for Dr. Reynolds," Detective Cushing said.

"The doctor is not in," the woman said.

"What's your name?" Cushing asked.

The girl blinked, as if she was surprised by the question. "Um, my name's Gina."

"Well, Gina, where is the doctor today?"

"Gee, I don't know," Gina said, suddenly becoming more girl than woman.

"Would he be at home?" Cushing asked.

"He might," Gina said. "I really don't know."

Cushing looked at Jakes. He shrugged. They had Reynolds's home address, so he figured they might as well check there.

"Okay," Cushing said, leaving her card. "If he comes in, please ask him to call me so we can make an appointment to speak."

Gina took the card and said, "Um, sure."

"Thank you."

Jakes and Cushing turned to leave. At that moment, a middle-aged woman came rushing in. She looked like she had dressed in a hurry.

"What's this about my appointment being canceled?" she asked. "You can't do that with only a half hour's notice."

"Mrs. Jansen, please—" Gina said, but the agitated woman cut her off.

"I demand to see the doctor! This is . . . absurd! I cleared my schedule for this consultation."

"When did the doctor cancel?" Jakes asked her.

Mrs. Jansen hesitated, studied Jakes, apparently liked the looks of him and decided to answer.

"Less than a half hour ago," she said. "It's preposterous. He demands a week's notice, and then does this?"

"Have you seen the doctor before, ma'am?" Cushing asked.

"No, this was to be my first appointment."

"Mrs. Jansen, we can reschedule—" Gina started, but Jakes cut her off.

"So the doctor was in today, but he decided to leave?" he asked.

"Um . . ."

Jakes and Cushing turned and walked back to the desk. The girl shrank back in her seat. She looked around for help, but there didn't seem to be any. Mrs. Jansen stood back, confused.

"Gina, if you impede a police investigation, you can get in a lot of trouble."

"I-I'm not. I—"

"Doctor Reynolds did have office hours today, right?" Cushing asked.

"Y-yes."

"And he left abruptly?"

"Um, yes."

"Did he get a phone call before he left?"

"Th-the doctor gets a l-lot of phone calls," she stammered.

"Is there a nurse here?" Jakes asked.

"N-no," Gina said, "everybody's gone b-but me."

Her eyes filled, but she managed to hold back the tears.

"Gina," Cushing said, "if I were you, I wouldn't call the doctor after we leave. Do you understand?"

"Y-yes."

"And if I find out you did, I'll come back to arrest you—with handcuffs. Understand?" Cushing was getting into it.

The girl's eyes went wide, and she nodded.

As they turned, Jakes looked at Mrs. Jansen.

"Ma'am," he said, "you might want to find another doctor."

"Well," Mrs. Jansen said.

As they left, they could hear the woman once again berating the poor girl.

Chapter 28

"I think the doctor got a call warning that we were coming," Jakes said.

They got into the car and buckled up.

"That may be my fault," Cushing said.

"What do you mean?"

"I called ahead to see if the doctor was in."

"And you identified yourself?"

"I'm afraid so," she said, looking chagrined. "I'm sorry, I didn't think—"

"It's okay, Cushing," Jakes said. He was annoyed but didn't show it. She was feeling bad enough. "We'll find him. Let's just go check out his house."

"You really think he's going to be there?" she asked, starting the car.

"If he got warned off, no," he said, "but it's our only logical next step."

As they pulled away from the curb she asked, "You think Gina will call him?"

"Depends who she's more afraid of," Jakes said, "you or him . . ."

*   *   *

"So, tell me what you were thinking," I said.

"What could I think? I had only been to two places, and both were police stations."

"Did you mention the doctor's name at either?" I asked.

"No, but the sheriff knew. I had spoken with him on the phone from LA."

"So he could have called Dr. Reynolds and warned him."

"Yes," Jakes said, "or someone from his office. Or maybe he really didn't know until Cushing's call alerted him."

"What about his house?"

"Cushing and I went, but no one answered the bell. In fact, we couldn't get past the front gate."

"So you gave up?"

"I wanted to come back here and meet you," he said. "And Cushing had to get back."

"Are you and Detective Cushing going to work together again?"

"Probably," he said, wrapping his arms around me. "She's my police contact."

"You asked her if she was married or had kids," I said. "Did she ask you?"

"I don't think so."

"You don't think so?"

"We talked about a lot of things in the car, killing time," he said. "No, now that I think of it, she didn't ask."

"So when's your next date?"

"Date?"

"With Detective Cushing," I said. "How did you two leave it?"

He reached out and tried to pinch my side, but I pride myself on not having an inch to pinch, so he had to look elsewhere. He finally settled on my butt.

"She's going to run a background check on the good doctor for me," he said. "Of course, I had to tell her how to run an extensive one."

"She's a detective and didn't know how to do that?" I asked.

"She's computer literate, but most of her work is community service."

"Then why did they assign her to you?"

"Because I don't think they're really in a hurry to help me," he said.

He also reminded me that detective was not a rank in the Las Vegas Police Department, so she really did not have any training for the job.

"She's not going to get in trouble?" I asked.

"She just needs to sit at a computer and access a few official databases," he said. "She's allowed to do that."

"And what's your partner doing while we're here in Vegas enjoying ourselves?"

"Running background checks on Shana and anybody else he can think of."

"Thanks for this." I looked from his mouth to his eyes to all the candles.

"You've gotta go, right?"

"I promised Sarah I'd be back for dinner."

"What time am I going to see you tomorrow?"

"I finish the brunch at twelve. I'll be free for two hours."

He stood up, looking all sexy. Just then his cell phone rang. It was sitting on the bathroom counter next to mine. He flipped it open and read the caller ID.

"Davis?" I asked.

He shook his head.

"Detective Cushing."

"Oh, lovely. Go ahead and answer it."

He did, standing there stark naked, looking very hot, and listened for a few minutes. Finally, he said, "That's interesting. No, no, that's okay. I can meet you for dinner. Just bring those printouts. Okay. Thanks."

"What printouts? What dinner?" I asked, after he'd broken the connection.

"She's got some interesting information about the good doctor," he said.

"Like what?"

"I'll find that out when I meet her."

"Well, go and meet her, then. But dinner? Really?"

"You're unavailable. Remember?" He held my eyes. He didn't have to say anything else. I knew what he meant.

"Fine. Have dinner. Just don't do anything silly until we talk again, all right?"

We got dressed, and there was an awkward silence that lasted all the way until he dropped me off at the back door of the Bellagio.

"Have a nice dinner," I said. I didn't mean it one bit.

"I will." He kissed me. "But I'd rather be having it with you."

Chapter 29

I woke Saturday morning with a full schedule ahead of me. My mom had made plans with Sarah to go to Circus, Circus, then to the Excalibur to see the show. They left the room before I did. I was putting the finishing touches on myself when my cell rang.

"Morning," Jakes said.

"How was your dinner with Detective Cushing?"

"No dinner," he said. "At least, not with Detective Cushing."

"Why not?"

"She canceled, said she had something to do," he said. "So it was dinner on my own."

"What about her news?" I asked, smiling. "The printouts?"

"I'm meeting her at noon at a diner off the strip," he said. "For coffee. Wanna come?"

"Noon?" My brunch would be over at noon, but I could be a little late. He took my silence as hesitation.

"Don't you want to meet Detective Cushing?"

"Sure, I do," I said. "Okay, noon it is."

"Write this down."

He gave me the address of the diner.

"What are you going to do until then?"

"Go to the doctor's office on the off chance he's there," he said.

"Not many doctors work on Saturday," I said.

"Well, maybe I'll take a run over there anyway. After that, maybe some video poker until our meeting."

"You said you weren't a gambler."

"I'm not. But, hey, this is Vegas, baby."

"What are you *really* planning to do?" I asked.

"Okay, I thought I might check out his house."

"If he's not home—"

"I'm counting on that," Jakes said.

"What do you mean? You're going to break in?"

"It's the only thing I can think of."

"You can't do that," I said. "You're a cop."

"Not in Vegas, I'm not."

"But that's even worse," I reasoned. "If you get caught—"

"I won't."

"If you do, you could go to jail and lose your job," I said. "Is it worth the risk?"

"My job is to find out who killed Shana Stern," he said. "That's what I'm going to do, whatever it takes."

We both fell silent then. I could hear him breathing. I'd heard that sound before, when we would lie close together in bed.

"I want to come with you."

"Oh, no, Alex—"

"Oh, yes," I said. "At the very least, you'll need a lookout."

"Lookout?" he asked. "You've been watching too many—"

"Don't make fun of me, Jakes!" I said, cutting him off. "I came here to help, remember?"

"Okay, okay. You're right. I didn't mean to make fun of you."

"Go and meet with your new . . . partner," I said. "Hopefully, she'll have something helpful to tell you."

"And you go and meet your legion of fans," he said. "They're probably waiting eagerly. I'll bet if Davis wasn't working, he'd be here at this thing."

"Oh, I get the feeling his allegiance may have changed a bit," I said.

"I don't think so. To him you'll always be Tiffany."

"Maybe that's the problem."

"Alex, I'll see you a little after noon."

"I'm looking forward to meeting your new . . . friend."

"I like this jealous side of you," he said. "I like it very much."

"You wish."

Chapter 30

I reminded Larry, my driver, that I needed to be picked up at noon; then I stepped out of my limo in front of the Las Vegas Hilton and was met by a handful of very eager event organizers. Poster-sized photos of all the actors lined the entrance to the hotel, and a red carpet had been laid for us to walk on. What a nice touch. It also worked as a "trail" for us to follow to the Grand Ballroom, where that morning's brunch was to be held.

"I love your dress, Alex! How are you this morning?" Kathy Tomson was Daytime in the Desert's organizer. She was in her element planning events like this. She also doubled as a fan-mail answerer. If she worked for you, she would pick up your fan mail from the various soap opera production offices and go through the letters. Then she'd send you a list of names to sign on photos. Any special requests, such as birthdays or, sadly, notes for fans who were ill, and she'd let you know so you could write something personal to them. I always admire people who are good at what they do and do it with grace. Kathy

Tomson is one of those people. That's why I use her for my fan mail.

"I'm fine, Kathy. How are you? Are you managing to have any fun this trip?" As we headed down the red carpet, we passed a massive photo of my smiling self. I had expected a throng of screaming fans, but I guess they were already inside.

"Oh yeah. If you call winning a couple grand at keno fun." If Kathy wasn't a big keno fan before, she sure was now.

"You're kidding me. Good for you. How do we look inside, anyway? Did you get a big turnout?"

"You know, it's funny. We all know that ratings are slipping. And viewership is down, down, down. But the soap fans are really loyal and enthusiastic. So the short answer is yes. There's probably seven hundred people this year."

She led me to the back entrance of the ballroom. There were about fifteen other actors waiting in a lineup. "Alex, they'll announce your name. Just go through that curtain and have a seat on the dais. Have fun, and I'll see you inside." She left to, I assume, corral more actors.

"Oh, hi, Brad. Hey, Priscilla. How is everyone?" What the heck was Priscilla wearing, anyway? It was nine o'clock in the morning and she was dressed in a full-length beaded gown. She was known to be a little out there and always took the whole Soap Opera Glam thing a little too far. But I shook that off and said hello to the rest of the actors, introducing myself to the two or three I had never met.

"Hey, Alex. Where are you staying, anyway? We're all on the same floors at the Bellagio," Brad said. "Word has it you got special treatment. Should I be pissed? How'd you swing that?" Word got around. It was like being in high school again. So much of life was, after all.

"I guess the manager likes me. Sorry. You want to come over and look at it? I'll let you play on my grand piano!" I teased. Brad was a nice guy and meant no harm.

"No worries! I guess I'm fine in my puny little suite. So, you want to hear a bad-beat story? I'm in the poker room last night. I've got wired aces. I'm bluffing my ass off trying to reel the table in. So far—"

Brad was interrupted by the last of the actors straggling in to line. One of them was Andy McIntyre from the *Tide*. I was surprised to see him. I wasn't sure he was still working that much. We gave each other a big hug. I missed him.

"Alex. It's great to see you. Nice dress. How's Sarah?" Andy asked.

"She's great! Thanks for asking. How are you?"

"Oh, you know. Hangin' in there." He lowered his voice. "I've been promised a big story. Hank is going to have a near-death experience. Problem is, I don't know whether he lives through it or dies because of it." Hank was the character Andy had played on the *Tide* for many years. There was sweat on Andy's upper lip. I hoped he had saved his money; it didn't sound so good.

"It'll be great. Maybe an Emmy, huh? You always bounce back." I hugged him again. We went so far back it was scary. And I genuinely loved the guy.

Just then I heard Kathy's voice over a microphone, welcoming everyone to the fan breakfast. A roar of cheers and applause broke out when she mentioned the actors who were here for the event. Then she began announcing our names.

"And we have Priscilla Schmidt from *The Bare and the Brazen*!" Applause again as Priscilla walked out through the curtains. No matter how many times I had done this sort of thing, it was always a little nerve-racking. I guess that's what made it fun.

"From *The Bare and the Brazen* and, not so long ago, *The Yearning Tide*, let's hear it for Alexis Peterson!"

I straightened my dress and pushed through the velvet curtains. Kathy wasn't kidding. The room was filled with a sea of cheering fans. Tables had been set up and breakfast was being served. I took my seat at the long table on the stage facing the audience. I waved and said hi to some familiar faces. The rest of the actors were introduced, and once we were all seated, Kathy announced the rundown for the entire day.

They began showing clips and highlights from the previous year of both shows. I was looking out across the room, half expecting to see Randy's face. He had done that to me last year at an event at the Television Academy. I breathed a sigh of relief. No Randy. That I could see, anyway.

We actors chatted among ourselves as we were

served a not-so-delicious breakfast of sausage and scrambled eggs. At least the coffee was good. Kathy got up and began a presentation of awards fans had voted on. There was Best Couple, Best Villain, Best Heroine/Hero and Best Story Line.

"And for Best Story Line, Alexis Peterson. Felicia and Fanny." Whoops! That was unexpected, and I had a mouthful of scrambled eggs. I quickly swallowed and got up. Kathy passed me the mike and a plaque.

"Thank you all so much. How kind. I had a blast playing both characters. Thanks for your support, and I hope you have a great time this weekend." I sat back down as they cheered.

The rest of the morning went off without a hitch. Kathy knew what she was doing and it showed. We finished the award ceremony, our plates were cleared and Kathy came up to let us know our limos were waiting outside the back entrance of the kitchen.

No rest for the weary. I gave the limo driver the address of the diner where I was supposed to meet Jakes and Detective Cushing.

I wondered if she knew I was coming, or if I was going to be a surprise.

Chapter 31

I sat in the car and heaved a sigh of relief. These events were draining. But I had entered Limo World. That's the place where you pour yourself some ice-cold water in a crystal glass, check yourself in the lighted mirror, adjust the AC and find your favorite station on the stereo. I didn't even bother watching the route that we took to get to the diner.

When he stopped in front of the coffee shop, I got out. I told Larry I had to be back at the Hilton by two, so maybe he could pick me up at one thirty. I had an outfit in the limo and I'd make a quick change in the talents' green room before the signing. Jakes had said to meet him inside, and he was there waiting for me at a table . . . alone.

"Where's your friend?" I asked, sitting down across from him.

"She'll be here by twelve fifteen," he said. "I wanted a few minutes to talk with you alone."

"About what?"

"First, how did your morning go?"

I told him about the award I had received, and

then we ordered coffee and got on with why we were there.

"After I hung up with you this morning, I decided not to try the doctor's office."

"But, Jakes—"

"I intend to case his house tonight instead. I want to get a look inside that house."

"Does he live far from here?"

"No—maybe twenty minutes. In an extremely upscale community called Lake Las Vegas. It's pretty impressive."

"Shouldn't you get a search warrant?" I mean, if you can, you should always play by the rules, right?

"No probable cause, especially since I'm not in my own town and don't know the judges here. So I have to get a look at the house and the grounds in the daylight before I break in tonight."

"What do you want me to do?"

"Just what you said you'd do," he answered. "You'll be my lookout. We'll have to rent a car—I don't want to use mine—and then you'll stay behind the wheel and hit the horn if you see anyone."

"Anyone?" I asked. "Anyone at all?"

"Anyone suspicious," he said.

I started to feel nervous. We were planning a caper.

"Come on," he said, reaching out and touching my hand, "it's not like this is the first house you've entered illegally."

"Those weren't really breaking and entering," I said.

"What were they, then?"

"Okay, maybe they were," I said, "but not in a strange town. If we get caught, we're going to jail, buddy."

"So the key is not to get caught," he said.

"Look," I said, "I know you're a good cop, but I don't know that you're a good burglar."

"I'm a great burglar," he said. "Don't you know cops make the best criminals?"

"Why's that?"

"Because we learn on the job," he said, "and we learn from the best."

"You're not going to tell Detective Cushing about this, are you?"

"No," he said, "I don't want to make her an accessory."

Fine, I thought—I get to be the accessory. I guess maybe I should have been flattered. And he was right: I had broken into a couple of houses during my short amateur-detective career. So why was I so nervous this time?

"Here she is," he said, standing up. "Detective Cushing."

I turned in my chair to have a look at Jakes's new friend.

Chapter 32

Wow.

She was beautiful.

Jakes was either blind or stupid to have described her the way he did, and I preferred not to think he was stupid. Attractive in a stern kind of way? Was he trying to spare me, or did he really see her that way? If he did, he was the perfect man.

"Detective Cushing," Jakes said, "meet Alex Peterson."

"Ms. Petersen." She looked surprised. "I know you. I watched *The Yearning Tide* when I was in college! I had no idea . . ." She stopped and extended her hand. "Sorry. It's a pleasure."

She wasn't really gushing, but spoke rather slowly in a perfect, richly modulated voice. Damn, I thought, she could have her own phone-sex line.

"It's nice to meet you," I said. "Jakes has told me so much about you."

"Jakes?" she said, with a frown.

I shrugged. "It hardly seems right to call him anything else."

She looked him up and down. "I guess you're right."

"Have a seat," Jakes said. "Let's get some coffee, and you can tell us what you've found."

He waved for the waitress.

"Us?" Cushing asked. She still looked confused. I had the feeling our little meeting was Jakes's way of introducing me into the equation he'd already formed with her.

"Yes," he said. "Alex and I came to Vegas together to investigate Shana Stern's murder. I told you she was the one who found the body."

"Oh yes, you did mention that," she said. "I just didn't know . . . well . . . that you two were, uh . . ."

"A couple?" Jakes asked. "Yes, we are. But Alex has also been very valuable when we've had cases involving, uh, show business."

"I see." I wasn't sure she did, but at least she saw that we were a couple. "And this involves show business?"

"Shana, the vic, was an actress, as well as a former Playmate," Jakes said. "And her ex-husband is an actor."

"Ah," she said, "I see." And maybe for the first time, she did.

"In any case," Jakes said, "anything you have to tell me, you can say in front of Alex."

She took out a printout and placed it on the table.

"What's that?" Jakes asked.

"Take a look."

Jakes picked it up, started to read it. His face changed and he leaned in and started again.

"What is it?" I asked.

He was still reading when Cushing answered.

"I decided to check the computer for unsolved murders of young women. Of course, there's no shortage of those, but I found this one interesting."

I looked at Jakes. "What's interesting about that one?"

He looked at me. "Same drugs in her system."

"Antibiotics and painkillers?"

"Yes."

"But that doesn't necessarily connect this one girl—"

"That's not what killed her," he said. "Her throat was cut, same as Shana's."

I sat back in my chair. "So Shana wasn't the first."

"No," he said. He looked at Cushing. "Any more?"

"If there were, I would have brought them," she said, "but I can widen the parameters of my search. Henderson, Boulder City, even Laughlin and Reno."

"Do it," he said, then added, "please."

She nodded.

His cell rang at that point. "Excuse me. I've got to take this."

He got up and walked toward the restrooms, leaving Detective Cushing and me alone.

"Ms. Peterson—" she said.

"Alex, please."

"I'm Debra," she said. "May I ask some questions?"

"Personal or professional?"

She shrugged. "A little bit of both."

"Sure, why not?"

"Are you and Jakes . . . serious?"

It seemed like such a simple question, but I guess Jakes and I hadn't really talked about it. Were we serious? He hadn't really been involved with my family. But did I want it to be serious?

"Yes," I answered honestly.

"I see."

"Any other questions?"

There probably were, but Jakes returned before she could ask them.

"Something important?" I asked.

"That was my partner," he said, sitting down. "He was letting me know that he has nothing."

"So what do we do next?" Cushing asked.

"We?" Jakes asked.

"We're in Vegas, Detective," she said. "You don't really have anything without me."

"This is my copy, is it?" he asked, touching the file.

"It could be."

"Family info in here?"

"Yes."

"Then I need to talk to the family of the dead woman," he said.

"And for that you need me," Cushing said.

"And me," I chimed in.

They both looked at me, but I returned Detective Cushing's look.

"Sorry," I said, smiling sweetly, "but where he goes, I go."

Cushing looked at Jakes.

"That's true," he said.

"Okay." She gave in. "When?"

"How's right now?" Jakes asked, looking from Cushing to me.

"Fine with me," Cushing said.

"And me," I said. I still had an hour before I had to be back at the Hilton.

"Detective Cushing?" he said. "Your car?"

"Sure," she said. "Why not?"

Chapter 33

The family's name was Bronsky, but the dead girl's name was Linda Bronson.

"That's what the girls out here do," Detective Cushing said from behind the wheel. "Change their names when they go onstage as showgirls."

"Change their names," I said from the backseat, "and get new boobs?"

"Right. Unless she was in one of those all-natural shows." She locked eyes with me in the rearview mirror. I wasn't sure how I had ended up in the backseat. Maybe as cops, they were just used to their positions up front. But Jakes had told me that Cushing usually rode a desk. I guess I should have called shotgun.

"How long ago was this girl found dead?" I asked.

"Two months," Cushing said.

"And no others?"

"No. Not until LA, I guess."

"Shana," I said.

"The only connection we have is the way they were killed," Jakes said. "If we can connect her to Reynolds, then we have another link."

"So how do we do that?" I asked. "We can't find the doctor."

"We'll find him," Jakes said, "but until we do, we'll talk to the family, see if they know anything about Reynolds."

"You may have a problem there," Cushing said.

"What do you mean?" he asked.

"You haven't read the whole file," she said. "She moved out of her parents' house because they didn't want her to be a showgirl."

"So where'd she live?"

"With some other girls."

"I wish you'd told me that before," he said. "We should be going to see them."

I saw Cushing duck her head. I knew if I could see her face now, she'd be red.

"I'm sorry," she said. "I—I didn't think—"

"It's okay," he said, his tone softening the way it did with me sometimes. Maybe he just couldn't help sounding sexy, but I didn't like him talking to her that way. "We're already committed to this. We'll talk to the family and then the girls."

Cushing nodded.

"It's really okay, Cushing," he said, again. "I should've read the file."

He wasn't being sexy, I realized. He was being kind. Funny that it would be while I was listening to him talk to another woman that I would realize how much I loved him.

*   *   *

Spanish Hills was one of the largest custom-home communities in Las Vegas. "High-end homes owned by professional people." That was how Detective Cushing put it.

"Mr. Bronsky," she said, "is a very expensive dentist. The community is gate guarded, and the homes run an average of fifty-four hundred square feet."

"You sound impressed," I said.

She looked at me in the rearview mirror.

"My parents live in a community like this. No, I'm not impressed."

She showed her shield at the guard gate, told the uniformed rent-a-cop that she was there to see Dr. Bronsky. The guard made a call, but gave Cushing a pass only after Jakes displayed his shield, as well. They both introduced me as an associate.

We approached the front door of the Bronsky home. Since Cushing was the legal one, we let her knock and take the lead—for the moment. I was sure that once inside, Jakes would ask the questions.

The neighborhood seemed middle-class, the house a ranch that had probably been built in the fifties. Cushing had pulled her car into the driveway, behind a four- or five-year-old Chevy Malibu.

The middle-aged woman who opened the door radiated waves of sadness. She had to be the mother who had recently lost her child.

"Yes?"

"Mrs. Bronsky," Cushing said, showing her badge, "my name is Detective Cushing; this is Detective Jakes and his associate, Ms. Peterson."

She looked at me curiously, and I hoped not to be recognized. It would have been intrusive.

"The police?" she asked.

"Yes," Cushing said. "May we come in and have a word with you?"

"Is this about my daughter—" she started, but a man's voice cut her off.

"Where's the damn tape, Alice?" he demanded.

"It's there, dear," she said, "with the other boxes."

"I can't find— oh, there it is. What the hell was it doin' there?"

The woman's shoulders tensed up for a moment. She seemed embarrassed.

"Yes, ma'am," Cushing said, as if the man had never interrupted. "It's about your daughter."

"Very well," she said, backing away from the doorway. "Come in, then."

"Thank you," Cushing said, and walked inside.

Jakes stepped aside so I could follow, and then brought up the rear. As the woman closed the door behind us, we stepped through a small entry area into a living room filled with boxes, some sealed, some open. A heavyset man in his fifties was struggling to tape one of the boxes closed.

"Goddamn it, I told you to buy the brown tape—" He saw us and stopped. He straightened, leaving the dispenser on the box, and frowned.

"What's goin' on?" he demanded.

"Dr. Bronsky, I'm Detective Cushing; this is Detective Jakes. He has some questions—"

"What kind of questions?" the man demanded.

"Who are you people? What happened to Detective Childs?"

"Detective Childs is still working on the case, sir," Cushing said, "We're just doing a follow-up—"

"I only talk to Childs," Bronsky said.

"Sir," Jakes said, "what's your first name?"

"Charlie," Bronsky said, then, "Charles. But I prefer you continue to call me Doctor."

"That's fine, Doctor," Jakes said. "I'm not a Vegas cop; I'm from LA. We have a dead girl in my town who may have been killed by the same man who killed your daughter."

"When?" Bronsky demanded.

"A few days ago."

"The son of a bitch is in LA?" he demanded. "Is that where Childs is?"

Jakes cut Cushing off before she could answer.

"No, sir. The Vegas police knew nothing about it until I came here and told them. I asked for their help, and they assigned me Detective Cushing."

"Why the hell wouldn't they give you Detective Childs?" Bronsky demanded. "He knows all about my daughter's murder."

"Well," Jakes said, throwing the entire department under the bus, "I guess he was too busy—"

Bronsky's face turned so red, I thought he was going to explode.

"Dr. Bronsky," Jakes said, "if we can sit down, maybe I can explain."

Chapter 34

Jakes got Bronsky to sit and calm down. Then he actually got some intelligent words from him. It probably helped that Cushing and I kept quiet and allowed Jakes to handle it. Unfortunately, the man didn't know that much.

"We lost her," he said, shaking his head, "when she moved out and mutilated her body."

"I'm sorry?" Jakes said. "Mutilated?"

"Those phony . . . things," Bronsky said, holding his hands out in front of his chest.

"You mean . . . she had plastic surgery?" Jakes asked.

Bronsky looked like he had tasted something bad. "You can't call that surgery. She just couldn't be happy with what the Lord gave her, could she?" he complained.

I looked around the room again. It was obvious the Bronskys were moving. On one wall was the outline of a crucifix. Getting breast implants and becoming a showgirl might have been Linda Bronsky/Bronson's way of distancing herself from her religious upbringing. At least, from her father's point of view.

When Jakes asked the Bronskys questions about Linda's life after she left home, they pleaded ignorance. In fact, Dr. Bronsky said he didn't speak to his daughter once she moved out.

"She wasn't my daughter anymore," he said. "Not once they got hold of her."

Jakes didn't bother to ask who *they* were.

Mrs. Bronsky led us to the front door, still with a sad, faraway look in her eyes.

"I guess, judging from the boxes, you're moving?" Jakes asked.

"Yes," she said. "My husband doesn't feel we can stay here after what's happened to . . . to our daughter."

"He can't put all the blame on Vegas," Cushing said.

Jakes and I exchanged a look, but said nothing. Mrs. Bronsky just shook her head and closed the door.

As we got back to the car, I said to Jakes, "I'm impressed."

"With what?"

"The way you handled the father," I said. "I didn't think we were going to get anything out of him."

"We didn't," Cushing pointed out.

"Yes, but that's because he didn't know anything," I pointed out, "not because he wouldn't talk."

"Alex is right," Jakes said.

"What about the wife, though?" Cushing asked. "Doesn't a mother usually know more about her daughter than a father does?"

"You'd think," Jakes said. "But I got the distinct impression this woman was totally clueless."

"The father complained about his daughter's fake breasts," I said. "He seemed more upset about that than he did about her death."

"Men like that . . ." Cushing said, but allowed it to trail off.

"Men like that . . . what?" I asked from my back-seat position.

She started the car, and then abruptly turned the engine off.

"I'm sorry," she said, "but that man reminded me of my father. They're the same—bullies hiding behind their religious beliefs. My mother had the same look as Mrs. Bronsky. I knew as soon as we walked into that house."

"That couldn't have been easy for you," I said.

"I'm sorry," Jakes said.

Cushing waved a hand and said, "I shouldn't let my emotions interfere with my work."

"A good detective knows how to put her emotions to good use . . . Detective," Jakes told her.

She didn't answer.

Chapter 35

I was running—I mean, literally running—down the hall of the Hilton to the Grand Ballroom, where the question-and-answer session was being held, trying to tuck my blouse into a very tight pencil skirt while holding a pair of Manolos in my right hand. I had called the limo driver from the backseat of Cushing's car. She had given me a location where I could change cars. She and Jakes went one way; the limo and I, another.

I'd tried to change my clothes in the limo but had not quite finished the job. That made me nuts. I was a good twenty minutes late and I hated that. I prided myself on being punctual, and now here I was, feeling like I had let Kathy and all the fans down. An assistant saw me and met me at the door.

"I'll take you in through the rear entrance."

"I'm so sorry I'm late! I'm Alex. What's your name?" I was out of breath.

"I'm Theresa. And I kind of know, I mean, ha, ha, ha. I know who you are—for sure I know who you are. Like, it's okay. It's fine. They just got started. Really. Ha, ha, ha, ha." I had to listen to her babble the whole way through a labyrinth of hallways, through the kitchen and to a large metal door. "Right through there. Ha, ha, ha." The girl made me nervous, but I didn't have time to dwell on it.

"Thanks," I said, and flung open the door, assuming it would lead to a backstage area where I could finish getting dressed and then discreetly sneak onto the stage. But no. And hey, thanks, Theresa. There I was. Center stage. Bright lights. Barefoot. Blouse all untucked. Balancing shoes and purse. Trying to catch my breath. Smack-dab in front of about seven hundred fans. What could I do? I waved my Manolos.

"Well, look who decided to show up. Alexis Peterson, ladies and gentlemen." The fans clapped and whistled.

I had read in the itinerary that Brad was the emcee for this part of the event. And there he stood in front of the dais, about thirty feet across from me on the other side of the stage. He sauntered over.

"More important matters to attend to, Alex? Like maybe, oh, I don't know, getting dressed?" Everyone laughed.

I'm sure I was a nice shade of scarlet right about then, but what could I do? I grabbed the mike and said, "Oh, shut up, Brad. Instead of making fun of me, why don't you help me get dressed?" The crowd roared as I turned around and had him help me with the button on the back of my skirt. "Sorry I'm late, everyone. But I'm so happy to be here now." I

slipped on my pumps and strolled across the stage
to my seat on the dais.

"Now, that's an entrance. Ladies and gentlemen,
Alexis Peterson." Again, everyone laughed. I sat
down and was trying to collect myself when I heard
Brad ask if anyone had a question.

"You, over there in the lime green top. You have
a question?" Brad asked. "Could you stand up,
please?" An assistant handed her a microphone.

"Yes, I do. For Alexis. Um, why were you late?"

Of all the questions I was prepared to answer—
about boyfriends, ex-husband, family, costars; oh,
I don't know, murders, maybe—that wasn't one of
them. Brad handed me the mike and I just sat there,
dumbfounded. After a moment, I stammered, "I was
out seeing the sights. I love Vegas. Don't you?"

Brad took a question for Priscilla next. Someone
asked about her gown. It was another beaded number strangely inappropriate for the time of day and
weather. Apparently, they thought it was beautiful.
No accounting for taste, I guess.

A few more questions were asked, none directed
toward me, and I took a moment to look out at the
people in the crowd. The stage was a good six feet
higher than the floor of the ballroom, so I had a fairly
decent view. Lots of women of all ages, and, not surprising to me, lots of men, too.

A lot of people think it's a female phenomenon,
soap operas. But I knew better. Just as many men
as women watched the shows I'd been on over the
years, and wrote letters, too. I'd received fan mail

from all sorts of guys: cops, FBI agents, doctors, lawyers and, believe it or not, even priests. Soaps were many people's guilty pleasure.

I was looking around the room and thinking about what had happened earlier that day—Debra Cushing, the Bronskys—when I saw someone I knew sitting in the very back of the room. I gasped. Next to me, Hannah Varga from *The Yearning Tide* asked me something. I was in such shock, it took a moment to understand her.

"Are you okay, Alex?"

I smiled weakly at her and nodded; then I looked again. Sure enough, it was definitely the Stalker. Shana's stalker. I couldn't believe I hadn't noticed him before. He stood out like a sore thumb. I didn't know what his being here meant, but it couldn't be good. I wasn't sure how to handle the situation without causing a commotion. I certainly wouldn't want to scare all those people into a mass exodus where someone could get hurt. And I didn't want to scare him away. Maybe he knew something. Or even worse, maybe he had killed Shana, and I was next.

I looked around for security. There was a guy at the very rear of the room. I tried to get his attention quietly. Not easy when you're sitting in front of seven hundred people. I waved without lifting my arm, jerked my head, and contorted my body in weird ways. So weird that Hannah asked again, "Are you sure you're okay? Do you need a doctor?" I looked at her blankly. What was I going to do?

I did the only sensible thing a strong, independent woman does when in trouble. I called my boyfriend.

I was being discreet. Really, I was. I pulled my cell phone from my purse and I texted Jakes *Shana stalkr n blrm* and then *Wht shd i do.*

"Alex, are we keeping you from doing more important things?" Brad was back in front of me, stupid microphone in hand, obviously being an asshole. I jerked my head up and, wide-eyed, stood up. I didn't miss a beat.

"Are you a dad? I tend to think you're not. When you're a parent, you're on call twenty-four/seven. Yes, Brad, even during times like this. My daughter needs to know when I'll be back to see her. And I was just trying to let her know with a text."

Awwwwwwww! the fans said in one voice. I nodded to them. We all understood one another. God help me for using my daughter in a lie, but I was desperate.

"Of course, Alex. Parenthood is the most important thing of all." And gratefully, that pain in the butt moved on to his next victim.

I, however, was stuck trying to figure out what to do. He was still there, staring straight at me with his squinty pirate eye. I got chills; he freaked me out so much. Maybe he was trying to figure out a way to get to me and slit my throat? Would he pull out a gun and shoot me? Was I over-the-top paranoid?

Beep, beep, beep. I jumped in my seat and looked down at my cell *very* discreetly. It read, *Wher n rm?*

I quickly texted back, *lst tabl by bk dr on lft*. I hoped it made sense. Thank God for cop boyfriends. Just then, two security guards opened up the rear door of the ballroom, looked to the right and the left and then, with great precision, walked up to the stalker, picked him up by both arms and hustled him to the doors. But he wasn't going quietly.

"Genesis 1:27! Genesis 1:27!" he screamed at the top of his lungs. Not that again.

Chapter 36

Fans were getting up from their tables, everyone speaking in hushed tones. Kathy had a cell phone in one hand as she took the microphone from Brad.

"Everyone, take your seats, please. Take your seats," she yelled out. "Everything is fine."

People were shouting out questions: "Who was that?" "Is there a problem?"

"Everything's under control. The man they took out of here was wanted for questioning by the Las Vegas police. Everything is fine." She looked over at the actors murmuring among themselves.

"Why don't we start the autograph signing? If the actors would please go sit at their individual signing tables, we can get started." She was clearly a little nervous, but covering well.

My new best friend Theresa led me to a table with my name on a placard.

"What was that about, huh, Alex? Scary stuff! That guy was probably a stalker. It happens at these things, I've heard. Ha, ha, ha. I've never seen it myself, but I've heard." Frankly, she seemed like she was one step away from being a stalker herself.

"Can you excuse me for a second, before we start? I need to make a quick phone call." I stepped into a corner of the room and called Jakes. He picked up immediately.

"I'm here in the Hilton security room, Alex. We're questioning that guy. Are you sure he's the same one that was at the Playboy mansion?"

"He's a little hard to forget. I'm positive. What's he saying? What does he want?"

"We just started questioning him. Did he say anything at all before he was taken out? Before the guards got to him?" Jakes was talking in a hushed tone.

"Yes! The same thing he was yelling at Hef's: Genesis 1:27. Over and over again. What do you think it means?"

"He's probably just a loony tune, a religious nut, but I'll have Cushing look up the verse and see if we find anything."

I hesitated.

"She's with you right now?" I couldn't believe, with everything going on, I was bugged by that.

"Yeah. Why?"

"Nothing. Just curious." Riiight. "What should I do now?"

"Just stay the course. Do your thing. What time do you finish?"

"I'm done here at"—I looked at my watch and it read three forty-five—"five o'clock. I was going to go back to the hotel for a couple of hours and see Sarah and Mom before the cocktail party at seven, but if you need me . . ."

"No, you go ahead. Where will you be at nine? I'll pick you up."

"The Hilton. In the back, by the kitchen entrance. You're sure you don't want me to talk to this guy with you?"

"Yes, Alex, I'm sure. I'll see you at nine. Oh, and wear dark colors tonight. Just in case." And he hung up. Just in case of what? I was left wondering as I put my cell away and went back to my table. Besides developing a cramp in my right hand from signing autographs for an hour, the rest of the afternoon was uneventful. Thank God.

"Mom! We had so much fun at Circus Circus. Look what I won." Sarah thrust a giant clown at me. I had a deep-seated distrust of clowns, but I didn't tell her that.

"Wow. That's awesome. How'd you do it?" I asked while trying to avoid getting too close to the stuffed toy.

"She played the ring toss about four hundred times. That clown cost fifty dollars. But it was worth it. Wasn't it, Sarah?" my mom chimed in. She was looking a little frazzled and worse for the wear. I felt bad.

"Hey, Mom, why don't you lie down for a while? Maybe get room service. I have an hour and a half before I'm needed again. I want to take Sarah out to dinner. We'll be back around six thirty."

"I *could* use a little rest." She gave us both kisses and headed for her room, using the wall for support. Suddenly, she looked, dare I say, old. "Let's go, Mommy. I'm really hungry. Can we eat by the pool?" Sarah, on the other hand, had all the energy in the world.

"Sure, sweetie pie. Go run and put your suit on and we'll go."

I put mine on and off we went. What was wrong with me? Had I been so busy I hadn't even noticed how tired my mother was? Maybe I was expecting too much from her lately.

Chapter 37

I have to say, it felt great relaxing in the Jacuzzi after the day I'd had. Sarah jumped in the pool and then the Jacuzzi as we waited for our chicken fingers and French fries to arrive.

After about fifteen minutes, a waitress set down two large plates on the table next to our chaises. We both toweled off before we snuggled up to eat. I learned a long time ago that kids' menus always have the best comfort food. We were both enjoying our fried-food extravaganza when suddenly Sarah asked me something I wasn't the least bit prepared for.

"Why don't you have a boyfriend, Mommy?" You never know what's going to come out of their mouths!

"Why do you ask me that now, sweetheart? What's going on?" Kids and their parents sat by the pool. Maybe that had gotten her thinking.

"I don't know. I just think maybe you miss Daddy sometimes. 'Cuz I do." Oh no. The dreaded *D* word.

I grabbed her and wrapped my arms around her.

I couldn't help but tear up. I just kept hugging her. Finally, I could speak.

"I'm so sorry, honey. I'm sure you miss Dad. Sometimes adults do stupid things, ya know? And little kids get hurt by those stupid things." I turned her to face me. "Are you feeling sad?"

"No, not sad. Well. Maybe. A little. I just really want you to have someone that you love. And maybe I could have a baby sister. We could share my room, and I'd share all my dolls and stuff. I promise." Whoa. She'd really thought this out. "I know not Daddy or Paul, but maybe there's someone else you could love."

Oh, my God. She was worried about me. Kids are amazing. I looked her in the eyes and said, "I love you so, so much, little girl. And don't you worry about me. I'm just fine. We both are." Maybe I was trying to convince myself.

I guess it was time. Decisions would have to be made when we got back home, and I couldn't pretend any longer. I needed to make some changes. Big changes. No matter how much it hurt. I couldn't help but feel I was shortchanging the most important person in my life. And come to think of it, myself, too. I kissed her head and said, "Let's get back to the room and order room service dessert for you and Gramma. Want to?"

"Yayyyy!" We grabbed our stuff and headed up.

I threw on a little black dress (I know—a cliché, but I did), grabbed some black sweats for my "caper," kissed Mom and Sarah and ran down to meet Larry the limo driver.

I spent the next two hours mingling with fans and sharing small talk with the other actors. A lot of talk was about the stalker. Who was he? Why was he at the hotel? In Vegas?

"Hey, Al. Did you know that dude they pulled out of the signing? Hannah said you were acting strangely right before security came in." Brad had sidled up to me.

"No, not one of mine." I tried to change the subject. I just didn't want to go into it with Brad. "Hey. You did a good job today. And an even better job harassing me, too."

"Sorry about that. You were a pretty easy target." He stopped a waitress who was walking by. "Could you get me a shot of Patrón, Gold if you have it? What do you want, Alex?"

"Just a mineral water. Thanks." Off she walked toward the bar.

"Mineral water? You don't need something stronger at these things?"

I laughed when suddenly a drunken woman from—I looked at her name tag—Missouri grabbed Brad and put him in what seemed to be a head-lock. He looked at me with *Please rescue me!* eyes. I just smiled weakly and waved good-bye as he was dragged across the room.

Things were getting crazy in there. Booze, fans and drunken actors. Uh-oh. I looked around and happened to notice that Priscilla was doing an impromptu solo dance number in the middle of the room. She had completely outdone herself in the dress department. She was sporting a full-length, skintight white gown. It appeared to be a little see-through if she stood in the right light. And she had on a tiara. What was she thinking? I had no time to be judgmental, though, because my cell beeped. A text from Jakes.

Cn u cm now? Im outside. It was almost nine o'clock—well, eight thirty. Close enough. Everyone seemed to be enjoying themselves. Nobody had me in a headlock, so they'd never notice if I left a little early, right? I deftly made my way to the back wall of the room, opened the farthest door, where the least amount of people were, and was just squeezing out into the kitchen hallway when someone called my name.

"Hi, Alexis. Where you goin'? If you're looking for the ladies', like, it's on the other side of the ballroom. Do you need something? I just wanted to say how much fun I'm having. I love these events." It was my pal Theresa.

"Hi, Theresa. Actually, uhhh . . . I'm feeling a little under the weather. I thought I'd go back to my hotel and get a good night's sleep."

"Oh. You can't go. Wait! I never got a picture of you today." She pulled out a small digital camera.

"Okay. Go ahead." Theresa took a couple of photos.

"Just a couple more. Like right inside here." She was trying to pull me back into the ballroom. She really was annoying.

"I'm just going to sneak on out of here. I'll see you tomorrow at the breakfast, okay?" I kept trying to close the door behind me, but Theresa wasn't letting me go. Finally, I had to physically push her away—and right then, the flash on her camera went off. Great. She had a not-so-flattering photo of me brutalizing her. I hoped she wasn't on Facebook. If she was, I was doomed.

Chapter 38

Jakes picked me up in back of the hotel in a rented, dark, three-year-old Pontiac.

"Nice wheels," I said, getting in.

"It was the most discreet-looking thing I could find. Hey, look at you. Black works," he said, taking in my black sweats. Despite what my friend Theresa had said about the ladies' room, I'd managed to find one between me and the back door and had made a quick change. I tossed the bag with my dress in the backseat.

"What? Isn't this what stylish lady burglars are wearing these days?"

"Yeah," he said, "if you're Catherine Zeta-Jones . . . or Alexis Peterson."

I didn't mind the comparison.

"Let's go," I said. "The caper awaits."

He laughed, started the car moving and said, "You're really into this, aren't you?"

"Yeah. Is that bad? Truthfully, I am a little scared."

"I can take you back and do this myself," he said, calling my bluff.

"No, that's okay," I said. "You need a lookout." And I didn't want to take any chances it would end up being Detective Cushing.

"So, what happened with the stalker?"

"We had nothing to hold him on, Alex, so we had to let him go. But I think he's harmless."

"He doesn't look harmless," I said. "He looks creepy and crazy."

"That may be, but I think he's just a crazed fan— my partner amped to the ninth power."

"No, you're wrong on this one. Davis is nothing like that guy. I know fans and I know crazy. There's a difference."

"Maybe you're right. Anyway, I warned him, maybe even scared him a little," he said.

"What did he say about that other thing?" I asked. "The Genesis thing?"

"He didn't say anything," Jakes said. "Couldn't get him to talk."

"How did you let him go? I mean, where—"

"I had security walk him out of the building; told them to hassle him if he came back in."

I nodded.

"Cushing looked up the Bible passage. Something about God creating man and woman in his own image. Why would he be spouting that?"

"I don't know," I said. "Which version did she look it up in?"

"King James, I think."

I decided not to talk about her anymore. Didn't want him to think I was jealous.

We drove in silence for a few minutes. And then I asked, "Is this what you and Davis do for each other? As partners? Back each other up?"

"Hell, no," he said. "Davis would never do this, and he'd never stand for me doing it. My old partner, though—my longtime partner—he and I did whatever we had to do to solve a case."

"And how many cops like you are there on the force?" I asked.

"Are you asking me how many cops bend the rules?" he said. "I can't answer that. It's up to each individual how far they want to go to solve a case."

"And how far do you go?"

"To solve a murder, I go all the way, Alex," he said. "It's the only way I know how to do things."

I flashed on a bathtub full of bubbles and a bottle of champagne on ice in his motel room. He wasn't lying.

"How did your day go?" he asked.

"Very well, considering," I said. "But I'm more interested in your day. What did you and Detective Cushing do after you dropped me back at the hotel?"

He took a quick glance over at me.

"You know what we did. We went to see the roommates."

"Well," I said, "we're going to be in the car for a while, so why don't you tell me how it went?"

"Okay," he said, "I'll tell you exactly how it went. . . ."

Chapter 39

Linda Bronson, née Bronsky, had shared a condo just off the strip with two other girls who worked with her at the Riviera.

"Susan Couture and Elizabeth Sessions," Cushing told Jakes, "are about the same age as Linda was, twenty-five. That's not exactly young for a showgirl. There are plenty of twenty- and twenty-one-year-olds working the casino shows these days. The Riv is starting to show its age, so that's apparently the only place these girls were able to get jobs."

"I thought the Riviera was a legend in Vegas," Jakes said. "One of the last vestiges of the Rat Pack–era Vegas."

"That's what I said," Cushing replied. "Aged."

"Okay, so you're saying these girls are not top showgirls."

"Far from it."

"So maybe they'd be going to somebody like Dr. Reynolds for help?" Jakes asked.

Cushing nodded and said, "That's what we're here to find out."

*   *   *

The condo had an underground parking lot. Jakes and Cushing rode up the elevator to the fourth floor, found the unit they wanted, and rang the bell. Cushing used her cell phone to call the Riv and find out if the girls were working that night. She was told that both were off on the weekend. She rang the bell a second time.

"Maybe they're out on the town," Jakes said. "Don't showgirls do that when they're off?"

"I wouldn't know," she said. "But my guess would be they'd be resting when they have time off."

"Let's hope you're right."

Jakes was about to ring the bell again when they heard the locks turn. The door opened as far as a chain lock would allow, and one bleary blue eye looked out at them.

"Can I help you?"

"Are you Susan or Elizabeth?" Cushing asked.

"I-I'm Susan," the girl said. "Who are you?"

Both detectives showed their shields.

"We'd like to come in and ask you a few questions about Linda Bronson."

"Linda?" Susan said, her eye widening. "L-Linda's dead."

"We're here about her murder, Miss Couture," Jakes said. "Let us in."

"Oh, uh, all right," she said. "I'll just— all right."

The door closed, the chain came off and then she swung it open. Jakes and Cushing entered and closed the door behind them.

"Where's your roommate?" Jakes asked.

"She's . . . out," Susan said.

She stood there in a shapeless blue terry cloth robe, arms folded across her chest. Jakes couldn't tell if she had a showgirl's body or not. Her face was pretty, even devoid of makeup, but he thought she looked older than twenty-five. She seemed to have the crow's-feet of a thirty-five-year-old.

"I'm sorry," Susan said, running her fingers through her mussed-up blond hair. "I was asleep."

"Is that what you girls do on your days off?" Jakes asked. "Sleep?"

"What else is there to do?"

"Go out on the town?" he asked.

She laughed humorlessly. "Who's got the energy for that?"

"Can we sit?" Cushing asked.

Susan waved them to the furniture, which looked secondhand. The building itself was upscale enough, but it obviously took three of them to make the rent.

Cushing and Jakes sat on the sofa while Susan took the two-cushion love seat.

"Is that what Linda used to do?" Jakes asked. "Sleep when she had some free time?"

"Sure," Susan said with a shrug. "I guess."

"Was it one of her days off when she was killed?" Cushing asked.

Susan hugged herself and said, "Yes."

"Did you do things together?" Jakes asked.

"No."

"Why not?"

"We weren't friends, not that way," she said. "Just . . . roommates."

"I see," Jakes said. "So that's why Linda was alone that night?"

"She wasn't supposed to be," Susan said, barely mumbling.

"What?" Cushing asked.

Susan raised her head and said, louder, "She wasn't supposed to be alone. She was . . . meeting someone."

"A date?" Cushing asked.

"No, she said she was just . . . meeting someone."

Cushing frowned.

"That's not in the case file," she said, more to Jakes than Susan. Then she turned to Susan and asked, "Why didn't you tell the investigating detective that?"

Susan shrugged again, rubbed her arms.

"Susan, are you feeling all right?" Jakes asked.

"Yeah," she said, "I'm just . . . tired. And my . . . my face hurts." She touched her cheek. "I—I think it's a tooth, or something."

"So, why didn't you tell the investigating officer about Susan meeting someone?" Cushing asked, pushing the girl.

"He didn't ask, I guess," she said.

"Okay, well, we're asking," Jakes said. "Who was she meeting if it wasn't a date?"

"I don't know."

"Man or woman?" Cushing asked.

"I don't know."

"Where were they meeting?" Jakes asked.

"I don't know!" Susan said. "I don't know anything. She just said she was going out to meet somebody. I told you, we weren't friends like that."

"What about your other roommate?" Cushing asked. "Elizabeth? Would she know?"

"I doubt it," Susan said, "but you'd have to ask her that."

"And when will she be home?"

"Tomorrow," Susan said. "She'll be home tomorrow."

"So, there's nothing else you haven't told the police?" Jakes asked.

"No," she said. "I don't think so." She hugged herself and rocked. Her body language said two things: one, she was sick; two, she was lying.

"Susan," Jakes said, "do you do drugs?"

"Drugs?" She seemed shocked by the question. "No, of course not. We're tested at work, randomly. If we're caught doing drugs, we get fired."

"When were you checked last?" he asked.

"About a week ago. I was clean. I mean, except for some prescription medication I take for pain."

"What kind of pain are you referring to?" Jakes asked.

Susan hesitated long enough to get Jakes's attention.

"Girl stuff. You know. Menstrual."

"Are you lying to us about something?" Jakes asked.

"Lying? Why would I lie?"

Cushing looked at Jakes, who shook his head. He didn't want to push her at that moment.

"Okay, Susan," Jakes said, "Detective Cushing is going to give you a business card. If you can think of anything else we should know, give her a call."

Cushing took the hint and produced a card. Susan took it, squinted at it.

"What's this mean, *Community Relations*?"

"It's just a title," Cushing said. "Just call and ask for me."

"Okay."

Jakes stood up. Cushing followed. Susan walked them to the door.

"We'll probably come back to talk to Elizabeth," Jakes said.

"We'll both be at the Riv tomorrow," Susan said. "You better come there."

"All right."

At the door, she leaned against the doorjamb and asked, "Should I not mention you were here?"

"No, you can tell her," Cushing said, after a nod from Jakes. "No harm in that."

"A-all right."

"Go back to bed, Susan," Jakes said. "You look like you need some rest."

She nodded, smiled weakly and closed the door.

Chapter 40

Out near the car, Cushing said, "Something's wrong with that girl."

"Yeah," Jakes said, "she looks wiped out. She needs some sleep."

"I've been wiped out, too," Cushing said, "but it doesn't make me look ten years older."

They got in the car, slammed the doors.

"I noticed that," he said. "You know what does that to a person?"

"Drugs?"

"And booze," Jakes said. "Or both."

"What do you think she's using?" Cushing asked.

"That's the problem," Jakes said. "No blood-shot eyes, no shakes, her nails weren't bitten to the quick. Whatever's bothering her is something else entirely."

"Why didn't we ask her?"

"Because we're going to talk to the other girl, Elizabeth, first."

"Why don't we look for her now?"

"Relax, Cushing. Tomorrow will be soon enough,"

Jakes told her. "We know where she's going to be. I have to meet Alex tonight."

"Oh."

Cushing started the car.

"She's very beautiful," Cushing said as she drove.

"I know."

"She was once voted most beautiful woman on daytime TV," she said. "In fact, I think it might have happened twice, but I'm not sure."

"I'll ask my partner," Jakes said. "He knows those kinds of things."

"Is he a fan of the soaps?"

"More than a fan," Jakes said. "He's a soap nut."

"Big fan of Alex's?"

"He was until she left *The Yearning Tide*. He kind of took it personally, but he'll get over it."

"She left the show?"

"Didn't you know? I thought you watched it."

"I did, until I got this job. I was hooked for a long time, but once I was fully employed, I managed to break the habit."

"I guess any kind of addiction is bad for you."

"Is yours?"

"What?"

"Your addiction," Cushing said. "Is it Alex?"

Jakes thought about that for a moment, then said, "I guess she is."

"But you said addictions are bad."

"I guess I just proved myself wrong."

"So you're in love with her?"

"Oh yes," he said, "I am."

They drove in silence for a few moments, and then he said, "Take me someplace I can rent a car—a discreet kind of car."

"But I can drive you—"

"No, you're done for the day," Jakes said. "I'll rent a car for the rest of the night. Alex and I have plans."

"Sure."

"Then you can pick me up at my motel tomorrow morning. Alex is going home with her mother and daughter. You and I, we're going to the Riv to talk to the other roommate."

"I can get back on the computer tonight," she said. "I'll just do some surfing. You never can tell what you'll come across."

"You going back to work now?"

She shook her head.

"I can do it from home," she said. "I've got my laptop linked to the department computer."

"They know about that?"

"They don't have to."

Jakes laughed and said, "I'll make a detective out of you yet, Cushing."

Chapter 41

I stared at Jakes.

"What?" he asked.

"She asked you if you were addicted to me?" I said. "And if you were in love with me?"

"Well, yeah," he said, shrugging. "What's the matter? You don't like my answers?"

"Your answers were very . . . sweet," I said. "I don't think I like the questions."

"Oh, Alex," Jakes said. "She was just making conversation in the car, the way partners do."

I stared at him again.

"What?" he asked, truly puzzled.

"You're such a man," I said. "Continue."

Jakes had decided to go visit Barry Stern, Shana's ex-husband, without Cushing. He wasn't sure how he was going to play it, and didn't want to have to consider Cushing if he decided to play bad cop with the ex. He didn't need a good cop along.

Barry Stern lived in a condo that was located right across the street from the Rio hotel, on West

Flamingo Road, just a couple of blocks off the strip. The doorman told Jakes he wouldn't find Mr. Stern at home that time of day.

"Where would I find him, then?" Jakes asked, showing his badge. "I know he's not in LA, working on his show."

"At this time, try the Rio," the man said. "You might catch him before he moves onto the Strip."

"And what would I find him playing?" Jakes asked. "Poker?"

"Naw," the man said. "He ain't got caught up in all that. He plays blackjack."

Jakes thanked the man, got in his car and drove across the street.

The Rio was decorated in a Mardi Gras motif. If Jakes had gone into the back section, he would have seen tracks in the ceiling for the Masquerade Show in the Sky. But he didn't have to go that far to find the blackjack tables.

When Shana had been killed and Jakes found out she had been married to an actor from *The Bare and the Brazen*, he had gone to his computer and looked him up on IMDB. Sure enough, a couple of recent photos had been posted. So when he checked the blackjack tables at the Rio, it was easy to find Stern sitting at the last one, seat three. Seats one, two and four were empty.

Jakes came up alongside him just as he busted out of a hand by drawing a fourth card.

"Take a break," he said.

Stern looked at him.

"You kiddin'? I'm just about to get hot."

"It'll have to wait."

"Who says?"

Jakes showed his badge.

"You're not in your backyard, Detective."

"I'm branching out."

The dealer, an old guy who looked like maybe he'd dealt Billy the Kid a hand or two, was waiting.

"Deal," Stern said.

"Don't," Jakes said. He looked at Stern. "Let's talk."

Stern's matinee-idol face—peppered with lines that made an actor distinguished and an actress desperate—scrunched up into a look of distaste.

"Is that the only way I'm going to get to play?"

"Looks like it."

He slid a twenty-dollar chip over to the dealer.

"Keep my seat warm," he said.

He slid off his stool and started to walk with Jakes.

"Where are we goin'?" Stern asked.

"This is your turf," Jakes said. "Aim for the bar."

"This way."

When they were sitting at the bar with coffee in front of Jakes and a beer in front of Stern, Jakes said, "I'm here about your ex-wife."

"I talked to the police about that already," Stern said. "That was . . . a shame. Shana wasn't a bad person, just . . . a little hard to live with."

"You talked to my partner," Jakes said. "But since

I was here in Vegas, I felt we should talk face-to-face."

"Well," Stern said, "that's okay, except I don't know what I can tell you."

"You can tell me about Dr. Eugene Reynolds."

"Gene? What about him?"

"Shana was a patient of his, right?"

"Well, yeah, that's right."

"Do you know the doctor?"

"I met him when Shana decided to go to him. We became kind of close, me and Shana, him and his wife, Janet."

"What, exactly, did Shana go to him for?" Jakes asked.

"Well, she wasn't getting any younger, so she decided to, you know, get some help." He held his hands out in front of his chest.

"You went along with it?"

"Hey, I loved her."

"Loved?"

"Yeah," he said. "Things went bad after that."

"Because of Reynolds?"

"Yeah, but not for the reason you'd think. After he did her breasts, she wanted more. I didn't want her to become addicted to the surgery, but she wouldn't listen. Later, she needed painkillers more and more. I didn't know why she needed them, but I helped her get them. When I realized she was getting hooked on them, I kept them from her. That's when we . . . parted."

Jakes figured that was why Alex had found so many bottles in Barry's dressing room.

"Amicably?"

"I tried to keep it friendly, but she was . . . changing. She was angry all the time, and nervous. She didn't want me around. I guess I should have tried harder. Maybe she'd still be alive. I'm sorry she's dead. I took some time off from work to kind of get over it."

"In a casino?"

Stern had the good grace to look embarrassed.

"This is what I do when I'm not working," Stern said. "Keeps my mind off . . . other things."

"Other things?"

"You know," Stern said. "Problems. Uh, everyday things. You know."

"I know," Jakes said. "The kinds of things we all have to deal with . . . in our own way."

"That's right."

"Well," Jakes said, stepping down from his stool, "I've kept you from your game long enough."

"Oh, that's okay," Stern said. "Do you, uh, have any leads on who killed Shana?"

"One or two," Jakes said. "We'll follow them up and see where they take us."

"Will you be heading back to LA?"

"Yep," Jakes lied. "Probably in the morning. Thank you for your time, Mr. Stern."

Jakes put out his hand and Barry Stern shook it.

"What about you?" he asked. "Going back to work soon?"

"Oh yeah," Stern said, "later this week. Wouldn't want them writing me off the show."

"No," Jakes said, "you sure wouldn't."

Chapter 42

"Doesn't seem to me you got very much out of him," I said, when Jake finished his story.

"No," he said. "I'm sure there was something he wasn't telling me."

"Why didn't you pressure him?"

"If he does know something, I didn't want to scare him off," Jakes said. "I want him coming back to LA, where I have more authority."

"So when he comes back to work . . ."

"I'll press him."

"Then why question him here in Vegas at all?"

"If I thought he was clean after talking to him, I'd leave him alone," Jakes said. "But he's not. So I'll wait."

"You're pretty smart for a cop," I said.

Dr. Eugene Reynolds lived in an area of the city called Lake Las Vegas, surprisingly close to his office. As upscale as Spanish Hills had been, Lake Las Vegas earned the word *ritzy*.

It wasn't a gated community. It was *too* fancy for

that. The homes were hidden behind high walls, and had their own wrought-iron gates out front.

"How the heck are you going to break into this place?" I asked, as Jakes pulled up alongside the wall.

"I scoped it out already," he said. "We're parked under this tree, so nobody can see us. It's dark, but it's even darker right here. I'm going to climb over that wall and make my way to the house."

"What about alarms?"

"I'll be careful."

"And dogs?"

"I've got some ground round in my pocket."

I turned my head and stared at him.

"For real?"

"For real."

"I hope you lined your pocket with plastic first."

He smiled at me.

"The meat's in a Baggie, Alex. Don't worry. I won't ruin my jacket."

He unscrewed the bulb from the dome light and then opened his door to get out. I put my hand on his arm to stop him.

"What?"

"Are you sure I can't go with you?"

He closed the door.

"Can you scale that wall?"

"I probably could. I've done a lot of my own stunts." Then I realized just how stupid that sounded, so I said, "Okay, so that doesn't count. I've never tried to scale a *real* wall."

"Well, this one's ten feet high."

"Then how are you going to get over it?"

"See that tree?" The huge tree we had parked under was outside the wall, not inside.

"Yes."

"The trunk is close enough for me to use both of them," he explained. "Don't worry. I'll get over it."

"What about getting back over it?" she asked. "You don't even know what's on the other side."

"I may have to find another spot," he said, "but I will. You stay right here the whole time. You can see the front gate from here. Anybody shows up, you call my cell and then drive away."

"What? Drive away? Why?"

"Because as soon as you call me you'll have to get out of here before somebody sees you."

"What about you?"

"Don't worry; I'll get out," he said. "But the only person who might show up is the doctor himself. Maybe that wouldn't be so bad, huh?"

"If he catches you in his house without a warrant—" I started, but he cut me off with a kiss—a long kiss.

"For luck," he said, leaving me breathless. "I'll see you soon."

"You better."

He zipped his dark Windbreaker up over his dark T-shirt, opened the door and got out, closing it quickly behind him. I moved over to the driver's seat to be near the horn and to see better.

I had to admit that Jakes moved gracefully. His black jeans and running shoes completed his burglary uniform. He hurried to the tree, braced himself between the tree trunk and the wall—back against the wall, feet against the tree—and began to move up the wall. When he got high enough, he was able to use branches to get on top of the wall. He paused there, and then either dropped to the other side or fell.

I wouldn't know which for a while.

Chapter 43

Later Jakes told me that as soon as he touched down on the other side, he knew he was going to have to find another spot to get back over. But that would come later. He flexed his knees and ankles, found them unharmed by the drop, then started to make his way across the vast lawn to the house. Luckily, he made it without encountering any dogs.

When he reached the house, he made his way to the front door. A quick check revealed, to his experienced eye, that the house was indeed alarmed. He was going to have to find another way in—another door, or perhaps a window.

It had also been Jakes's experience that wealthy people were cheap people. He'd known a lot of doctors and lawyers in LA who would alarm the first floor of their house, but not the second. It was stupid, and the alarm companies tried to tell them that, but there you go. They always thought the companies were just trying to hit them up for more money.

He hoped that a Las Vegas doctor would have the same attitude.

*   *   *

Dr. Reynolds's house turned out to be a "cracker box"—one that's easily opened. Jakes found a trellis in the back that led to a second-floor balcony. From there he was able to jimmy open a balcony door and enter the house.

He found himself in an upstairs library. Taking a small flashlight from his pocket, he began to search, moving on instinct. He'd know what he was looking for when he found it.

He quickly went through the room, which seemed to be strictly for show. Shelves were loaded with books, but there was nothing personal anywhere. Except for a box with some photos. He assumed they belonged to Dr. Reynolds. Photos with a dog. Dr. Reynolds in a lab coat—complete with name tag—surrounded by others in lab coats. Dr. Reynolds and another woman with Shana and Barry Stern. He wondered if that was because they were really friends, or if it was just the doc showing off his celebrity acquaintances. That one he put in his pocket.

From there he went into the hall and found the master bedroom. It was spotless, the bed made, bathroom towels dry. He went through the doctor's medicine chest, but found nothing.

There were other bedrooms upstairs, but they all had the same look—cold and impersonal. The doctor apparently wasn't much of a homebody.

He decided to go downstairs.

He took the stairs carefully, just in case the floor

was alarmed. Leave it to a cheap doctor to save money upstairs, but go top-of-the-line downstairs.

As it turned out, he didn't have to worry. There were no trip switches or infrared sensors on the first floor of the house.

He found the living room and dining room with no problem, but didn't waste his time searching them. He just kept on going until he found the good doctor's office. He checked his watch, saw that he had been in the house for more than a half hour. He worried that I had almost hit the horn several times already. After all, I was an amateur, but unlike most amateurs, he did not expect me to panic. He knew I had a natural talent for detective work.

Using his flashlight, not wanting to take the chance of turning on the desk lamp, he began to go through the man's desk. He found some files and personal papers, but all in all, there wasn't enough in the desk to indicate that someone actually did any business there. It was curiously devoid of any of the clutter usually found—used paper clips, rubber bands, business cards.

The desk itself was wood and metal; very utilitarian. Normally, anyone who spent significant time at a desk made sure it was comfortable and aesthetically pleasing. That one looked as if it belonged on a display-room floor.

There was a calendar. As he went through it, page by page, he found no notations anywhere. For a doctor, that guy didn't make any appointments.

There was an old-time blotter on the desktop,

which he found odd. It looked clean and new, had not been worn through in any spots or doodled on. Who kept a blotter and didn't scrawl at least a phone number? After all, they were easily replaced.

He was about to switch off his flashlight and give up when he spotted something. A white corner sticking out of the left side of the blotter. He used his fingernails to grab it, then slid out a business card. It was expensively done, embossed in gold letters. He shined the light on it. It had Dr. Eugene Reynolds's name on it, and the name of something called the Whitney Institute. But the address was not the address of the doctor's office in Las Vegas.

The address was in Los Angeles.

Chapter 44

I almost hit the horn a half dozen times, but stopped myself. Each time it turned out to be a false alarm. I soon realized there was a bend in the road ahead, and cars slowed down for it. As soon as they reached the doctor's front gate, they would speed up again and go right by me without a glance.

I was jumpy as hell, and tried to calm myself by thinking about Sarah and my mother, but my mind kept going back to the same subject—Detective Debra Cushing. It was obvious that she had an interest in my man. That didn't sit well with me. I mean, okay, it's flattering when someone notices your sig other, but Cushing was just a little too beautiful for me to be comfortable with it. On the other hand, Jakes seemed oblivious to the attention—and her charms. Was he that much in love with me, or was he just another clueless man?

I had been with a handsome man before. Randy had always attracted the ladies, but the difference was that he knew it. They'd flirt, he'd flirt back, and then he'd just shrug and give me a *What am I to do?*

look. I had a hard time mustering up any positive thoughts about my ex. Except when it came to our daughter. When he had been around, he was a good dad. And as Sarah so painfully reminded me, she missed and needed him. I wasn't sure how that was going to work, but I realized now that it had to.

When the knock came on the window, I practically jumped ten feet—or would have if I hadn't been sitting in the front seat of a rented car. I didn't remember locking the doors, but I must have. So I unlocked them and Jakes slid into the passenger's seat.

"Let's go," he said.

"What did you find?"

"I'll tell you when we get away from here," he said. "Drive."

"To where?"

"Just away," he said.

"Do you want to   "

"Drive, Alex."

I drove.

We not only got away from the house, but from the neighborhood.

"Pull in here," he said, as we approached a large gas station. "You want some coffee?"

"Sure."

"I'll be right back."

I bit my lip as he got out of the car. It was driving me crazy wondering whether or not he'd found anything. He came back quickly with two vanilla lattes he'd gotten from one of those machines that had a dozen different flavored coffees.

"I pressed the wrong button," he complained. "Damn."

"Where to?" I asked,

"Let's just sit here a few minutes," he said. "I want to catch my breath."

"Dogs?"

"There weren't any dogs, but climbing back out was not as easy as climbing in. Or maybe I'm just getting old."

We were parked in an end spot, where we couldn't even see inside the gas station. We popped the tops off our coffees and sipped.

"So?" I asked at last. "Did you find anything?"

"That's the weirdest house. It feels as if nobody has lived there for, well, ever. There were some papers in his desk, but hardly anything else. Except for this."

He pulled out the photograph he'd found of the Sterns and Dr. Reynolds and laid it on the armrest between us.

"Oh, my God. That's the same picture I found in Barry's dressing room. So that's Dr. Reynolds."

"It doesn't really tell us anything else, however."

"How can you say that? It proves they knew each other."

"We already knew that," Jakes said. "When Barry was talking to me, he referred to Dr. Reynolds as Gene. You only use a nickname when you know someone. But we do have proof of what we suspect—that Barry is lying, or at least holding something back."

"Did you find anything else?" I asked.

He handed me a business card. I had just enough light to read it.

"What's the Whitney Institute?" I asked. "And why does he have a card with his name on it for a place in LA?"

"Two things I want to find out as soon as we get back," he said.

"Tomorrow?"

"You're going back tomorrow," he said. "I'll drive back Monday."

"Why?" I asked. "I mean, why stay the extra day?"

"We have to go to the Riviera to question the other roommate tomorrow."

"*We* as in you and Cushing?"

"Uh-huh," he said, sipping the coffee. "Hey, this stuff's not bad."

"She likes you, you know."

"What?"

"Cushing," I said. "She likes you."

"Come on."

"No. You either don't see it or you don't want to see it, but she does. And you can't lead her on."

"Look, Alex," Jakes said, "she knows I love you."

"A man in love," I said, "is sometimes an even bigger target."

"I think you're being silly," Jakes said. "She wants to help, and she wants to learn."

"Okay," I said. "Don't say I didn't warn you."

"Alex . . ." He didn't finish. We drove in silence for a while.

"You want this back?" I asked, holding the business card out to him.

"Hang on to it for me," he said. "We'll check it out when I get back to LA."

"*We* as in you and me, or we as in you and Davis?" I asked.

"Well, I guess that would have to be you and me," he said. "I can't very well tell Len where I got that, now, can I?"

Chapter 45

After a quick kiss in the car, Jakes dropped me at the Bellagio. I was going to be leaving the next morning, but not until "Breakfast with the Stars" closed out Daytime in the Desert.

"Be careful," I said as I got out of the car.

"Alex, I told you," he said, "you're making something out of nothing. Cushing just wants to be a detective."

"I meant, no more burglaries, Jakes," I countered. "Jeez, get over yourself."

I laughed, stepped back and closed the door. I could see him shaking his head as he drove off.

When I got to the suite, Mom and Sarah were both asleep. It was almost midnight, but in Vegas it's never too late to do anything, so I decided to take a bath before turning in.

After the bath, I curled up on the bed in a Bellagio robe and went through my purse, which I'd be changing the next day. I pulled out the business card Jakes had found. The Whitney Institute.

I toyed with the idea of opening my laptop and investigating online, but decided against it. The hot bath had sapped the last of my energy, and I was nodding off.

I put the card in my wallet, which would be going into the other purse. With my last ounce of strength, I filled out the room service card and hung it on the doorknob so that Mom and Sarah could have a big room-service breakfast in the morning. Then I turned off the light and fell right asleep.

Sarah was very excited when the breakfast cart arrived. She chattered to the bellboy about everything she'd done since arriving in Las Vegas. I tipped him extra because he not only listened, but also had a conversation with her.

After breakfast (well, coffee for me), I got dressed and told Mom I'd call her when I was done with the last event. Larry and I would swing by and pick up Sarah and her and then go straight to the airport.

"That's fine," she said. "I'm going to take Sarah down to see the dancing waters one last time."

"Yay!" Sarah cheered.

"Have fun," I told them, and left.

I walked into the Grand Ballroom, which was set up with a breakfast buffet. Amid the fans and actors milling around, I saw Brad trying to flag down a waitress. He looked a little worse for wear.

"What's up, Brad? Late night?"

"You don't want to know, Al. You don't want to know." Then to the waitress, "Bloody Mary, please?

You know, on second thought, hold the tomato juice. Just vodka with a lime twist. Fast." She walked away with her eyebrows raised.

"What happened to you? I mean, after the head-lock," I asked.

"Oh, after the fan dinner, one of the waitresses asked me to go to a club that was rockin'. So stupidly I went. What can I say? She used to be a show-girl. Nice bod. We had fun." I got the impression he was going to go into detail about exactly what kind of fun he had.

"TMI, Brad. TMI." I didn't need to know any details.

I had heard enough. I waved a hand at him, rolled my eyes and went looking for my table.

It was a nice breakfast and the fans were all very happy. As I ate my scrambled eggs, I saw Priscilla. She was wearing a chiffon cocktail dress. At nine a.m. Frankly, her taste was kind of growing on me. Maybe it was time to go home.

Chapter 46

"So, how was it? And why didn't you take me?" George was using a curling iron a little too close to my face.

"Hey. Watch it!" I exclaimed.

"Sorry. Not really. How was it?" George asked again.

"It was fine. Busy." I studied his face in the mirror, and then it dawned on me. George was hurt. "Are you mad at me?" I asked.

"Why would I be mad at you? Oh, maybe because I've been there for you during all your crises and all your last-minute needs, and the second you get a real boyfriend, you dump me?" I couldn't believe what I was hearing. Was he serious?

"Well, if you are mad at me, maybe you can put the very hot curling iron down and we can talk about it." I winced as the hot wand came perilously close to my cheek.

"Your hair's done, anyway," he said as he put it down. His whole body kind of sagged.

I led him out of the room into the empty hallway.

In a hushed tone, I said, "I'm sorry, Georgie, if I hurt your feelings. I didn't realize."

"I just never hear from you anymore. You didn't tell me you were going to Vegas, either. I figured you were doing that thing that girls do—get a serious boyfriend and dump their friends." I was dumbstruck. "Wayne and I go through our ups and downs, but I'm always there for you." I felt awful!

"I'm so sorry. I didn't mean to." Had I really done that? Very possibly I had been all caught up in Jakes and murder and had put George on the back burner. Come to think of it, I hadn't even seen him since Hef's party. "I'm really, really sorry. You're my best friend. If I neglected you, I didn't mean to."

"It's okay. I just needed to get it off my chest."

"Well, let me make it up to you. I'll take you out. When are you free this week?"

"Wednesday or Thursday. I'm sorry if I was a little over-the-top. Silly! I guess I just need some girl time."

I hugged him. "Is everything okay with Wayne?"

"Yeah, yeah."

"I love you."

"I love you, too." He sniffled and went back into the dressing room.

I was heading down the stairs to the commissary to get a quick breakfast when my cell phone rang.

"Hey. I'm back. I missed you."

"That's nice to hear. How did it go yesterday?"

"Alex," Jakes said, "did you hear what I said? I missed you."

"I missed you, too." I said. "I'm sorry. I was being a little bitchy. In fact, I was a little bitchy the entire weekend."

"No, well . . . not the entire weekend."

"C'mon. This whole Cushing thing is annoying me."

"Really? Why?"

I couldn't believe him. Was he for real? "Never mind. What's going on? What happened yesterday?" I grabbed an orange juice from the refrigerator.

"I do have some bad news," he said. "Brass wants to see me today, so we can't get together until tomorrow."

"Are you in trouble—again?" I asked. "Could I get a bacon-and-egg sandwich on whole wheat, please?"

"Are you talking to me?" he asked.

"No. Sorry. One sec." I gestured to the cook. "Bacon and egg on wheat?" He looked at me, annoyed. And I didn't blame him. I hated when people talked on cell phones while shopping, ordering, driving. Guilty! "Well, what can they do to you?" I asked.

"I guess I'll find that out. Are you working tomorrow?"

"Yes."

"Can we have dinner afterward, then?"

"Yes," I said. "In fact, I'll cook for you. To make up for being so mean."

"And I'll let you," he said. "See you tomorrow night."

"Wait!" I said. "What happened in Vegas after I left? Did you talk to the other roommate?"

"We did. It was kind of strange, but it can wait until I see you."

"And what about the Institute?" I asked. "When are you going over there?"

"Probably tomorrow," he said, "but I won't know what I'm doing until after I have my meeting today. We'll talk about it all tomorrow, all right?"

"All right. I missed you."

"You already said that."

"I know. I thought you should hear it again."

He was quiet for a second.

"I missed you, too," he said. "Bye."

I finished my scenes earlier than I thought and was going through my bag when I found the business card from the Whitney Institute. Hmmm. Should I? Oh, why not. I called upstairs.

"Hey, George. Can you have someone cover for you and take off early?"

"Why?"

"Are you in the mood to do a little sleuthing?"

"Does this have to do with Shana's murder?"

"Yes, it does."

"Um, one second." I heard him talking to someone in the room. They went back and forth for a while. Finally, George came back on the line. "Let's go, Nancy Drew."

Chapter 47

"What are we doing in Bev Hills?" George asked as I craned my neck to see the addresses.

"I want to check out this Whitney Institute. It's supposed to be on Canon Drive. Ooh. There it is."

Turns out I didn't need the address. The building was midblock and stood out like the clichéd sore thumb. The architecture was modern, all white concrete and metal beams. Out in front was a large bronze sign on a slab of white concrete that said THE WHITNEY INSTITUTE. Underneath it, in smaller letters, FOR LONG-LIFE RESEARCH.

We drove around the block again, looking for the impossible: a parking space. Just when I thought I might have to valet at a nearby restaurant, one opened up. I eased my car in and put it in park. And there we sat.

"What now?" George asked. "Why are we here?"

"I'm not really sure, Georgie. Let's go in and snoop around."

"Wait. Don't you want to brief me? What should I say? Do I need another identity?"

"Don't get carried away. I just want to see if I can get some info on this doctor that Shana knew."

I reached for the handle to get out, then pulled back my hand. I knew Jakes would be mad at me for this, but we were already there, right?

The lobby was glass and marble. Sitting behind a marble partition at what was probably a very expensive desk was a woman who looked to be the double of the girl Jakes told me he had talked to at Dr. Reynolds's office in Las Vegas. She was probably twenty-five, with pale, perfect skin, clear blue eyes and delicately arched eyebrows. In front of her, in a half dozen little holders, were business cards of all the doctors who apparently had offices in the building. All white with embossed gold lettering, just like the one I had in my purse.

"Yes?" she asked. She seemed surprised that we were even standing in front of her. "May I help you?"

I looked from George to her, and I was stumped for a moment. What should I say I was there for? I wasn't even really sure what the Whitney Institute did. So I just threw it out there.

"I'd like to see Dr. Reynolds."

"Who?"

"Dr. Eugene Reynolds."

She looked puzzled. In an over-the-top, bad-acting kind of way.

"I don't think we have a Dr. Reynolds here," she said, indicating the collection of business cards in front of her. George didn't believe her, either. He covertly reached out and pinched my thigh.

"Ow! Oh, really?" I tried to cover my pain by bending down and getting a closer look at the cards. Kettering, Fischman, Cohen, Lyman, Sloan and Galloway. No Dr. Reynolds.

"See?" she said smugly.

I opened my purse, took out the business card Jakes had found in Reynolds's house, held it in front of her face and said, "See?"

She stared at it, and her eyebrows arched a little bit higher. She looked legitimately surprised.

"Oh," she said. "One moment."

She picked up the phone and dialed a number; she waited while it must have rung a half dozen times.

"Mr. Bennett? It's Julie, at reception. There's a woman and gentleman here asking for Dr. Reynolds." She listened for a moment, then lowered her voice and said, "I *did*, but she has his *card*."

She listened again, then said, "All right," and hung up.

"Mr. Bennett will be right with you."

"Mr. Bennett?"

"He's the administrator of this facility," she said, as if speaking to a child.

"Oh, doesn't that sound so very important," I said, before I could stop myself.

George pulled me away from her desk to wait—and to stop me from slapping her. He knew me too well.

Moments later, a man came walking down a winding staircase to the lobby. He was actually gliding more than walking, and wore a very expensive suit. I'd bet good money it was high, high-end custom and not off-the-rack. He had the same smooth young skin that the girl had. He looked to be about forty, and his dark, close-cut hair was peppered with gray.

"I want some of whatever he's having." George said under his breath. "We're not in Kansas anymore."

"May I help you?" he asked. His face didn't actually move when he talked. It was disturbing.

"I hope so," I said, assuming a haughty pose. "Your receptionist doesn't seem to know the names of the doctors you have on staff."

"And you were looking for . . . ?"

"Dr. Eugene Reynolds." I held the business card up in front of his face so he could read it, and then pulled it away before he could grab it from me. As it was, Jakes was going to be furious with me, even more so if I managed to lose the card.

"Ah, actually, Dr. Reynolds is not on staff here," Bennett said.

"Then why does he have a card?"

"Well, you see, we're a research facility," he explained. "Our doctors do not see patients."

"So then, why does he have a card? Why do these other doctors have cards?" I pointed out.

"Well, our physicians still need to identify themselves to other physicians, other researchers. May I ask where you got that card?"

I acted impatient. "Where do you *think* I got this card?"

He looked at me as if I was boring him to death. "Dr. Reynolds sits on our board of directors. He is very rarely even in this building, unless there's a meeting in progress."

"I see."

"Is there anything else I can do for you?"

"Yes," I said. "Just what kind of research do you do here?"

"Well, it's rather involved, but in layman's terms, I guess you'd say . . . antiaging."

"Antiaging? What kind of antiaging?" George felt compelled to ask.

Bennett looked at George as if he had just been bored to death a second time. "If you'll give me your names, I'll tell the doctor you were here looking for him."

"No, no," I said, "you've done quite enough. Thank you."

"You're welcome." He reached into his pocket and pulled out a card. He handed it to me, saying, "In case I can be of further assistance."

He didn't offer to see us out, didn't even wait for us to leave. He just turned on his heels and went back up the stairs.

"Excuse me?" It was Julie.

"Yes?" I answered, as I put the card back in my purse.

She crooked her finger at me, looking very contrite. I pulled George over to her desk.

"Yes?" I repeated.

"I'm sorry I was so rude, but I just realized . . . aren't you Alexis Peterson, from *The Bare and the Brazen*?"

"Yes, she is. And you *were* extremely rude to both of us. What makes you think you can treat people that way? Shame on you." George's bullshit meter had apparently topped off.

She lowered her voice. "I am so sorry. They train us to act a certain way with people. It's actually a job requirement." She looked truly embarrassed. And well she should be.

"That's okay," I said, hoping I could get her to talk more. "So, tell me, they don't see patients here at all?"

"No, not patients," Julie said. "But they use people in trial runs for certain formulas."

"Have you been worked on?"

"Well, I can't really say, but . . . oh, my God, are you considering being a subject? You will love the treatment here." She stroked the skin of her face and neck. "They can take *years* off. It's amazing. Not that you need it." She took a closer look at me. "Oh, well, you probably could use a little work."

"Can't we all, sugar? Can't we all? Well, except for you and your boss." George was getting slightly annoyed by her attitude. I needed to keep us on track.

"So, you've had the treatments?"

"Oh yes."

I leaned in and lowered my voice.

"May I ask how old you are?"

"I'm thirty-five." And proud.

I stood back.

"You don't look a day over twenty-five."

She smiled and said, "I know!"

"Okay, so they look good. If you like that *Stepford*, *Vampire Lestat* kind of thing," George was saying as I pulled away from the curb. "I really wanted to tickle that doctor and see if he would crack."

"Something's weird about that place, and it's got nothing to do with the receptionist. I know BOTOX when I see it, and that's all she's had."

"She obviously thinks you're considering joining one of their trials," George said. "Maybe she was just trying to help you decide. She seems to be a fan."

"Ya think?"

We drove in silence.

"Hey, Alex?" he said. "I think this whole thing with Shana got to me more than I realized at first."

"You mean finding her body?" I turned to look at him.

"Her being dead. I mean, one minute she was there with us, being a total diva, and then the next she was gone. It really made me think about how short life is. And how we just never really know what's going to happen. I think maybe I'm suffering from PTSD. I guess that's why I gave you a hard time. I just needed my friend."

"Oh, Georgie. I'm sorry if you thought I was blowing you off. I've been trying to figure out a lot of things lately."

"Anything you want to talk about now?" George said, ever the good friend.

"You're sweet." I sighed. "Anything *you* want to talk about now?"

"I think I'll save it for martinis and dinner later this week." We were pulling back into the studio.

"Okay. I'll see you tomorrow." I hugged him.

"Be careful, crazy girl."

"You betcha!" I smiled and watched him walk to his car.

Chapter 48

"Hold on a second, Jakes." I said. "Sarah's asleep; I'm closing her door." I made sure she was, and then sat down on the sofa with the phone and a glass of merlot.

"Go."

"The other roommate also claimed not to be that friendly with the dead girl, Linda. Didn't know who she was meeting or where." I was waiting with baited breath, but he didn't continue.

"And that's it?" I asked.

"Well, there was something odd about her."

"What?"

"Same as the other girl," he said. "Wrinkles around her eyes. Both girls look older than they claim to be."

"So either they were lying about their ages," I said, "or there's something going on."

"Well," Jakes said, "we know there's something going on. We just have to find out what."

That was when I said it.

"I think I have an idea."

"About what?"

"The Whitney Institute."

"I'm going to check it out tomorrow."

"Well . . . I went there today."

And that was when he said, "You did what?"

I grabbed my glass and went out onto the back deck, overlooking the canal.

"What were you thinking?" he asked urgently.

"To be fair," I said, "I was careful. I took George along."

"As a bodyguard? George? Are you kidding me?"

"That's mean. And unnecessary." The best defense is a good offense, after all.

"And you two lunatics went inside?"

"Well," I said, "Of course. We were there, so . . ."

"Jesus, Alex, you may have just painted a target on your back."

"I was just trying to help," I said.

"I told you I'd be going there tomorrow."

"Yes, but you have to show them your badge," I said. "You wouldn't have found out what I did."

"What did you find out?"

I told him about my first conversation with the receptionist, then my talk with Mr. Bennett and, finally, my last conversation with the receptionist.

"So the girl looks younger than she is, and the institute is studying antiaging?"

"Right," I said. "So maybe that's what Shana was going to Reynolds about. And the dead girl in Vegas. And what about those two showgirls?"

"They look older than they are, not younger," he pointed out.

"It's still aging," I said. "It's still a connection, isn't it?"

"Yeah, maybe," he said.

"So what are you thinking?" I asked.

"I'm thinking I'll still go to the institute tomorrow and ask around," he said. "But meanwhile, I'd like to have the two MEs—LA and Vegas—have another look at the bodies."

"For what?"

"Signs of aging—or antiaging. I don't know. If this is what we're dealing with, it's all getting kind of . . . science fiction–like."

"Antiaging is a big business," I told him. "Infomercials are running all night long, and every woman over twenty-five is looking for help."

"Well, you're not."

"I'm not getting any younger, Jakes," I said. "And believe me, high-def doesn't let you hide anything."

"Are you telling me you use antiaging products?" he asked.

"Of course! I've even been known to have chemical peels on occasion."

"Would you ever go to the extreme? A face-lift?"

"Not yet, but get back to me in five years. Getting older isn't easy. Especially on TV, in front of the whole world."

"I think you're beautiful the way you are. Inside and out. High-def, low-def—whatever."

"Thanks," I said. I think I was blushing.

"It's getting late. I better hit the sack. I have to see the chief tomorrow morning."

"Again?"

"It's just routine."

"You saw the brass today, you said."

"I saw my boss and his boss," he said. "Tomorrow I have to see everybody's boss."

"What's going on, Jakes?" I asked. "Are you in trouble . . . again?"

"I thought you'd know that about me by now, Alex," he said. "I'm always in trouble."

"Is this about going to Vegas?"

"Yes, I kind of . . . forgot to tell anyone at work that I was going."

"Jeez—"

"It'll be okay," he said. "I swear. So, when am I going to see you?"

"About that." I took a breath. "I was hoping you could come for dinner tomorrow night. With Sarah. And my mother."

"Really." He was quiet for a moment. "Really?"

"Yeah. Really. Be here at six o'clock for mac and cheese, salad, apple juice and, if you're lucky, a rousing game of Twister."

"I can't resist Twister. I'm there. See you tomorrow. Bye."

Before he could hang up, I quickly said, "I love you, Jakes."

"I love you, too. See you."

After Jakes hung up, I poured another glass of wine and walked outside. I stared out at the canals, remembering a killer drowning in what was essentially three feet of water. Jakes saving me. It was amazing I could even sit back there and relax. I tried not to dwell on it, though. I liked it here. And I *really* hated moving.

I had promised myself in Vegas I was going to make some changes in my life. One was to bring Jakes more into my daughter's and mother's lives. Having him over for dinner with the fam was my way of doing that. The second one was trickier.

Randy. How in the hell was I going to ever be able to be civil enough to him to let him back in my life, in any capacity? Even though I hadn't heard from him lately, I knew in my heart he wasn't going away.

Frustrated, I went back into the kitchen and put my glass down next to my purse. I caught a glimpse of something gold peeking out of a side pocket. I pulled it out and saw that it was the card Mr. Bennett had given me. It looked different from the one I had for Dr. Reynolds. It had the Whitney Institute and the address. But under it, in smaller letters, it read A SUBSIDIARY OF GENETICS SYSTEMS, INC.

I had to tell Jakes! I started to dial when I remembered he had said he was going to hit the sack. It could wait until tomorrow.

Chapter 49

The next morning I had the day off, so I dropped Sarah at school and then went to my favorite neighborhood grocery store. I walked in, and could have sworn that a couple of the cashiers looked at me funny. Was it because of the screaming match Randy and I had gotten into there recently? I wasn't a big fan of public displays of hostility, but whatever. They hadn't been married to the jerk.

I tossed my hair back and proceeded to get what I needed for dinner, even though I had said we would be having mac and cheese. That didn't mean it was going to be your garden-variety mac. Oh, no. I was going to show Jakes that my culinary skills were alive and well, and just screaming to be heard.

I found the gourmet cheese aisle and picked out some fabulous-looking Gruyère, Havarti, Parmesan and a couple of other, stinky cheeses, just for fun. I walked up and down the aisles and threw some of those curly noodles in the basket, a nice bottle of red wine, salad fixings, paper towels, toilet paper, lunch Baggies. And, of course, apple juice.

I walked to my car, wondering how I was going to find time to stop at Crumbs for some designer cupcakes for dessert, memorize my lines for tomorrow's show, help Sarah with her homework and make dinner. But then, I worried about those kinds of things every day. What I *didn't* worry about every day was finding a stalker sitting in the passenger's seat.

I had been looking down at my key ring, separating the ignition key. I opened the door before I even saw him.

"Please, Ms. Petersonnn," he said, in that weird way he had of talking. "I have to tellllll you. I was always tryin' to warn Shana, and now I'm tryin' to tellll you."

I juggled the grocery bags, put my hand inside my purse and groped for my cell phone. I was hoping he'd think I had pepper spray or something worse.

"If I could just talk to you. My name is Edddddie. I loved Shannnna."

I backed away from the car.

"Stop. You have to listen. I loved Shannnnna! I followed her everywhere."

"And now you're stalking me. I'm calling the police!"

That stopped him cold. He just looked at me with his squinty eye. His hair stood out wildly, as if he'd just gotten out of bed.

"I'm not stalking youuuu. You're no Shana. She was the perfect woman. You're nothing like herrrr. I know who killed Shannnnna."

A crazy, pirate-eyed, frizzy-haired stalker had just dissed me. I tried not to take it personally.

"What is it you know?"

"I saw everything."

Was he trying to tell me . . . ?

"Are you saying . . . you saw who killed her?" I asked. "You should be talking to the police."

"They don't listennnnn. They don't know. I found the answers in her trash and that's when I knew. It's up to Goddddd. Shana knew it. She had the papersss. Genesis 1:27. Genesis 1:27." He reached into his pocket.

Frightened that he was going to pull out a weapon, I made a dash for the grocery store. I don't think I've ever run a faster twenty yards in my life.

I bolted through the automatic doors and tried to close them with my fanny since my arms weren't free. Not advisable. It's like trying to move something in a dream. The more you push, the more resistance you get. When I looked out the window, I expected him to be right behind me. He wasn't. He was gone.

"May I help you, Ms. Peterson?" I looked around, and the same cashiers—plus a couple of shoppers— were looking at me with very concerned expressions on their faces. Had I become the crazy actress that lives down the lane?

"Uh, no. No. Just . . . no." I tossed my hair again and walked gingerly back out the door toward my car, glancing back and forth to make sure Eddie was indeed gone.

I went around the car, checking that Eddie wasn't hiding somewhere in the backseat. Finally, I popped the trunk and put the groceries inside; then I quickly got in the car and locked the doors. On the passenger's seat was a crumpled piece of paper. It hadn't been there before my encounter with Shana's "friend." Cautiously, I picked it up.

It was filthy, covered with smudges of chocolate and what looked to be ketchup. At least, I hoped it was chocolate and ketchup. Was he just leaving me a stinky present? My curiosity got the better of me and I unfolded it carefully. It appeared to be a business memo. I was about to crumple it back up and squirt a healthy dose of sanitizing gel on my hands when something caught my eye. At the top of the memo were the words *Gen.Sys. 1/27.*

"Is that where that Looney Tune came up with Genesis 1:27?" I asked myself. Reading down the page, I found that the memo explained, in very complicated terms, that a certain product was not to be used in trials anymore, due to certain detrimental effects on lab animals. It was signed by a Mr. Carl Bennett.

"Huh!" I gasped. Could it be? I pulled out the card I had been looking at last night. There, in beautiful gold lettering, was printed MR. CARL BENNETT, ADMINISTRATOR. And under, THE WHITNEY INSTITUTE: GENETICS SYSTEMS, INC. This was definitely a memo from the same guy. A memo dated January 27.

Chapter 50

I had to protect the memo. I looked around and realized that in the kid car, it wasn't going to be so easy. I rummaged in my purse and found my eyebrow tweezers. I used them to pick up the memo and hold it in the air. Then I remembered. I had just gotten plastic Baggies for Sarah's lunches.

I walked to the trunk and found the box in the grocery bag. I opened it with one hand and carefully placed the memo inside, then zipped it up.

"Ha! I'm getting good at this." I was frightened and elated at the same time. I was buzzing. I could just feel that the memo meant something. Something big.

"Jakes!" I shouted out to my Bluetooth. His cell kept ringing until it went to voice mail. "Call me back. I've got news."

I hung up, wishing I could just go downtown to the station and see him, but knowing that wasn't a good idea. He was tied up with the brass. I drove around a while, trying to figure out what to do. I decided, When in doubt, cook. So I headed home to do just that.

I threw the noodles in the pot of boiling water and had already started grating the different cheeses when my mother walked in from her guesthouse.

"Hi, Alex. Isn't it kind of early to be cooking dinner?"

"It is a little early. I guess."

She looked at me and then crossed her arms in front of herself. "Why are you doing all this?"

"Well. Because . . ."

"This is for a man, isn't it?" My mother was so smart about these things. She could have been a spy. Or a psychic. Or a mom. I took a deep breath, put down the grater and turned to face her.

"Not just any man, Mom. Jakes. I want you to get to know him. I want Sarah to get to know him. He's a good man. He's good to me. I want him in our lives. I know my track record stinks, but this is different."

She started to open her mouth, but I stopped her. "Okay, before you say, 'You always say that' . . ."

"I think it would be lovely to have Detective Jakes over for dinner. You don't have to please me. You have to please yourself. And you've been extremely careful and sensitive to Sarah's needs. Worry about your own for a change."

Startled, I grabbed her and hugged her.

"Okay, okay. Now, what can I do to help?"

I happily handed her the grater.

"Grate!" And she did. We did. I was having a hard time wiping the smile off my face when my cell rang. I grabbed it and saw it was Jakes.

"Finally! I've got big news!" I was about to spill it when I remembered Mom was in the room.

"What's going on?"

"Um. I can't say right now. Could you come over any earlier? Let's see." I glanced at the clock on the wall; it was three forty-five. "I have to get Sarah from dance class at four. I'll be back by four fifteen. Just head over here now."

"I can do that. Do you need anything?"

"Nope. Just you." Then I remembered. "Oh, and could you stop at Crumbs and get some cupcakes? Peanut butter chocolate for us, and whatever you like."

"I like the red velvet ones!" Mom piped in.

I looked at her and smiled, taken aback.

"My mom said she'd like a red velvet cupcake."

"Your mom said that? How can I refuse? I'll see you as soon as I can get there. Bye."

"Bye!"

I hung up the phone and dumped the noodles in the strainer, then into a casserole dish, threw the cheeses on top, added some butter and half-and-half. I was hoping I wouldn't cause any of us to have a coronary as I added bread crumbs for a finishing touch. I slid the whole thing into the oven and said, "Mom, I've got to get Sarah. I'll be right back."

Chapter 51

When I walked into the house, Sarah in tow, I was greeted by the most heartwarming sight. The French doors were open; a slight breeze was blowing in from the canals. The patio table was set with our "best" china (chunky dishes from Pottery Barn), candles were lit, classical music was softly playing on the Bose. And my mother and Jakes were out on the back deck, clutching wineglasses in their hands, both laughing their heads off.

I was such a sap for stuff like that. I teared up. Sarah ran out to join them.

"Hi, Gramma! Hi, Jakes! What's so funny? Want to see what I learned in dance class?" And she immediately did a pirouette, arms raised in a classic ballet pose.

Jakes got down to her level and said, "Wow, Sarah. You look like a professional."

"I want to be a dancer. Or a scientist. Maybe both."

"I like the way you think. How've you been?"

"Good. Are you staying for dinner?"

"He sure is," Mom said, and headed for the kitchen. "Speaking of which, I think it's ready."

"I've got lots to tell you," I whispered to Jakes as I followed my mother into the house. "It will have to wait until later, but you won't believe it!" He looked intrigued. And not very happy.

Mom and I put food on the table while Sarah and Jakes spent some time on the deck, talking about school.

"Okay. Dinner's ready!" I said.

We all took our seats. I have to admit, the mac and cheese looked pretty impressive. And tasted impressive, too.

"Mmmm! Mommy, this is so good. And so cheesy!"

"It is, Alex. Really good." Jakes said. "You can cook."

Everyone was passing the salad and bread and diving in. Conversation was light and easy. What had I been so wary of before? This was a cakewalk.

"Is Jakes your boyfriend, Mom? Are we going to have a baby sister?"

I almost did a spit take.

Jakes looked incredibly amused and seemed to really enjoy seeing me so flustered. It took me a second or two, but I went there.

"He is my boyfriend, Sarah. The baby-sister thing . . . We don't know about that quite yet."

"I'm glad. I like Jakes."

I looked over at Mom, and she nodded in agree-
ment. Jakes squeezed my knee under the table. It
was so, so nice.

The rest of dinner went very well, followed by the
cupcakes Jakes had brought. They were a very big
hit with all the Peterson girls. Jakes jumped up and
cleared the table and insisted on doing the dishes.
Another big hit with the Peterson girls. He wasn't
stupid! After a couple games of Twister that left us
all on the floor laughing, Mom and Sarah went into
her guesthouse to do homework and give Jakes and
me some time alone.

"That went well, huh?" I asked him as we got
comfortable on the sofa.

"Yes. Very. I like your mother. She's a hoot. And
Sarah. What can I say? She's amazing. You've done
a great job raising her."

"Thanks. I like her, too. She's a great kid." I looked
down at my wine. "And thanks for coming. It's nice
having you here. It feels . . . right." We kissed.

"So. What have you got to tell me? Did you do
something else stupid?"

"I resent that question. No, I did not." I stood up
and walked over to the bookcase, where I had put
the plastic Baggie with the memo inside. I handed
it to him.

"What's this?"

"Be careful when you open it." He looked from
me to the Baggie, then carefully unzipped it.

"What's on it? The stains, I mean."

"Chocolate and ketchup . . . I hope."

"Where did you get it?"

"It was in my car when I was at the grocery store."

"Yesss. And how did it get there?"

"This is where it gets interesting."

"What were you thinking?" he demanded, moments later.

"Why are you mad at me? It's not my fault Eddie came to see me. What should I have done?"

"You should have run as soon as you saw him," he said. "You should have called me right away. Or 911!"

"I did run. I was very careful. And I did call you! You weren't around." He was kind of pissing me off. "I didn't think of calling 911. Sorry. On the bright side, if I had called 911, we probably wouldn't have that." I pointed to the bag in his hand.

"And what is this?"

"Evidence."

"Of what?"

I groped for the right word, and finally came up with "Complicity."

"Complicity, huh?" he grumbled. "All right, let me take a look at this."

"Wait a sec. Why are you so mad?"

"I worry about you. When you're not with me. Okay?"

"Okay." I guess it was sweet. Kind of annoying. But sweet.

He turned the bag over so the memo fell onto the

coffee table. He then used the tips of two pens he produced from his pocket to unfold it.

"I suppose your fingerprints are going to be all over this thing?" he asked.

"I didn't know what it was until I opened it."

He read it.

"Genetic systems . . . unsafe formula . . . no approval . . . Gen. Sys. One twenty-seven?"

He looked at me and I nodded.

"Not Genesis 1:27," I said. "And look who it's signed by."

He peered at the signature at the bottom.

"Carl Bennett?"

I held out the business card that Bennett had so helpfully handed me.

"The Whitney Institute," he said, staring at the card, "is a division of Genetic Systems."

"Right."

He looked at the memo again.

"This is not specifically written to Dr. Eugene Reynolds," he said. "It's a general memo."

"But he must have seen it," I said.

"So you think this formula they're talking about—this botchuhylonic acid—has something to do with Shana's and Linda's deaths?"

"I'm saying that Eddie the stalker followed Shana everywhere, and he picked this up for some reason, and then made a point of giving it to me."

He sat back.

"That's not saying much," he said. "After all, the guy's lacking credibility. Don't you think?"

"Well, it's saying something. I can feel it. So what are we going to do about this?" I was adamant.

He leaned forward again, looked at the memo, tapped it a few times with one of the pens, then used the pens to fold it up as much as he could and slide it back into the bag. Made me remember how adept he was with chopsticks when we ate Chinese food.

"I'm going to have a talk with Mr. Bennett tomorrow," he said. "I'll confront him with this and see what his explanation is. I've also got somebody at Parker Center trying to find a residence in town for Eugene Reynolds."

"I'm coming with you."

"Don't you have to work?"

"I'll be done by ten a.m. Early day."

He studied me for a moment, then said, "Well, if you're with me, I won't have to worry about you and that crazy stalker having another rendezvous."

"That's not exactly what I would call what we had," I said dryly.

"I'll take this with me and have it dusted for prints," he said, tucking the Baggie into his pocket and standing up. I walked him to the door, linking my arm in his. "You did good, Alex. Nice work with the Baggie."

"Thanks. So you're not mad at me anymore?"

"I wouldn't say that," he replied. "But I'll still kiss you good night."

He kissed me in a way he couldn't possibly have kissed if he were angry.

"You made some points with my mom tonight," I said. "Also with Sarah."

"Sarah's easy," he said, "but your mother . . ."

"She likes you. I can tell," I said. "We'll do this again and again, and it will be known and accepted that we are . . . together."

"Is that what we are?" he asked. "Together? What kind of together? Baby-sister together?" Really? At our ages?

I pushed him out the door gently and said, "We'll talk about that later, too."

Chapter 52

Jakes picked me up at ten thirty a.m. We had breakfast at Du-par's in the old Farmers Market on Third
and Fairfax before we went to see Carl Bennett at the
Whitney Institute.

Over breakfast, Jakes explained to me how we
were going to explain my presence.

"I'm going to tell him that since you were there
when Shana was killed and discovered the body,
you've been assisting the police in our inquiries."

"Sounds like something from a bad script."

"Actually," he admitted, "I think I got it from a
Lifetime movie."

"He's going to think that I called you after I talked
to him yesterday."

"Maybe he will," Jakes said. "I want him to be nervous. Maybe he'll give something, or someone, up."

"Like Dr. Eugene Reynolds."

"If this is some sort of conspiracy to circumvent
the FDA, then somebody on the medical side has
got to be in charge. You said Bennett's not a doctor;
he's just the administrator."

"Right."

"Well, he's not going to want to take the fall for somebody else. And since he signed the memo, that's what I'm going to make him think. So go along with me."

"Okay."

As we left the restaurant and walked to his car, Jakes asked, "Have you told anybody else about this memo?"

I hesitated, then said, "Well, just George."

He gave me a stern look and said, "Okay, but nobody else."

After he left my house the night before, I had called Georgie to keep him in the loop. I didn't want his feelings getting hurt again. I told him about Eddie the Stalker, and about his leaving a clue behind. I didn't tell him exactly what it was, just that it could be something incriminating.

"Incriminating to whom?" he'd asked.

"Maybe the Whitney Institute," I'd told him. "Apparently they're trying to get some kind of medication approved, even though it might not be safe."

"Is it dangerous?"

"I don't know, Georgie. But Jakes and I are going to try to find out."

"Ooh, Detective McHandsome," he said.

I didn't tell Jakes about his new nickname, either.

"Drug companies are always bending the law to try to get formulas approved by the FDA," Jakes said as he drove. "They fly doctors to resorts for free vacations, buy them cars or simply bribe them with cash. If they get caught, they get fined. But you know what? They can afford a fine. It's just part of the cost of doing business."

"So they lie and they cheat," I said.

"And maybe steal," Jakes said.

"So, what are we thinking?" I asked. "That they murdered Shana, and maybe Linda, to keep anyone from finding out their formula didn't work? Would they go that far?"

"That's what we have to find out," he said. "Also, this whole antiaging thing . . . I'm having the MEs here and in Las Vegas go over the bodies again."

"Looking for . . . ?"

"A sign of . . . aging, I guess, or antiaging. Just something to tell us if those women had used some sort of medication that didn't work the way it was supposed to."

"I see."

"Oh, one more thing," he said. "Len is going to meet us there."

"Well, he is your partner."

"Just wanted you to know."

"How did he feel about your going to Vegas without him?"

"He wasn't happy," Jakes said.

"And how did it go with the big brass?"

"I'm looking at a possible suspension," he admitted.

"Jakes!"

"Don't worry," he said. "If I solve this, that'll go away. Especially if there are headlines involved. If we take down a major drug company, the brass will be very happy with me."

"A company like Genetic Systems?"

"Exactly." Happy, he put his hand on my leg. "And you're the one who came up with that clue. As mad as I was at you yesterday . . . thank you."

"So then, your bosses will be very happy with me, too?" I asked, putting my hand over his.

"Uh, no," he said, "they won't know anything about your involvement at all."

"You'll take all the credit?"

"I'll probably let Len have the credit," he said. "I'm trying to keep what you and I do together on the QT—if that's okay with you."

"I've told you all along," I said, referring to our relationship, "I don't want to get you into trouble with your bosses—"

"I know, and I appreciate—"

"—especially since you're so good at doing it yourself."

Chapter 53

We parked in front of the Whitney Institute and walked to the front entrance. As we entered, I saw the same girl sitting at the front desk.

"Where's Davis?" I asked.

"I don't know," Jakes said.

He wasn't out front, and he wasn't in the lobby.

"Come on," Jakes said, taking my elbow. "We'll start without him."

Julie looked up as we approached, and this time I rated a smile from her. It was short-lived, however.

"Ms. Peterson," she said. "Did you come back to make an appointment? You could have just called."

"Not exactly, Julie," I said.

"Miss, my name is Detective Jakes, LAPD," he said, showing his badge. "I'd like to see Mr. Bennett, please."

"Police?" Julie said, startled. She looked at me. "For real?"

I nodded.

She looked at Jakes, and he said, "As real as it gets. Homicide."

"Oh!" she said, grabbing at the phone. She used her French-tipped nails to pick out three numbers.

"Mr. Bennett? The police are here."

"Detective Jakes," Jakes reminded her.

"A Detective Jakes. He insists on talking to you. Yes, sir. I'll tell him."

She hung up and looked at Jakes.

"He'll be right down."

"Thank you."

Jakes was collecting the business cards on the reception desk and putting them in his pocket. I touched his arm as Bennett appeared on the stairs. He approached us, looking as vampirelike as ever, smiling and holding out his hand.

"Detective Jakes?" he asked.

"That's right."

"A pleasure, sir." They shook hands. "And Ms. Peterson. How nice to see you again."

"Mr. Bennett."

"What can I do for you, Detective?"

"I have some questions, Mr. Bennett," Jakes said.

"Very well. Ask them and—"

"I'd prefer to go to your office."

"Well . . . we really don't like to take people through the building, Detective," Bennett said.

"I'm not just people, Mr. Bennett," Jakes said. "Please lead the way."

Bennett looked distressed, but the skin on his forehead remained unlined. I was starting to think there was nothing mysterious about Mr. Bennett's appearance. Again, I knew BOTOX when I saw it.

"Well, all right."

He led us to the stairway he had used. Beyond that, we saw an elevator.

"What about the elevator?" Jakes asked.

"What?" Bennett looked at us over his shoulder. "Oh, my office is on the mezzanine. The elevator doesn't stop there."

Jakes looked at me and shrugged. I would not have even thought to ask that question. He was so cool.

Chapter 54

Bennett led us to a medium-sized office filled with modern, long, metal furniture. The room had no personality at all, which meant it matched Mr. Bennett perfectly. His desk was as unlined, unwrinkled, as the skin of his face.

"Uh, please, sit down," he invited. "I, uh, can't offer you anything. We're not used to having, uh, guests."

There were two chairs in front of his desk, so it seemed he was used to having people in his office at some time.

We sat down.

"I'm not a guest, Mr. Bennett," Jakes said. "I'm here investigating a homicide."

"Homicide? You mean . . . a murder?"

"I mean two murders, actually," Jakes said. "Two women who have one thing in common."

"What's that?"

"Dr. Eugene Reynolds," Jakes said.

Bennett stared at Jakes, then shook his head and said, "I don't understand."

"They were both patients of Dr. Eugene Reynolds. You know Dr. Reynolds. He's attached to this facility."

Bennett opened his mouth, then closed it. I thought he was about to deny it, but then he must have remembered he had admitted it to me.

"Dr. Reynolds is on our board, yes," Bennett said. "But we know nothing about his patients."

"But you know about him, right?"

"You mean, personally?"

"You know about his practice, what he does," Jakes said. "And you know where to contact him. Where he lives."

"He lives in Las Vegas," Bennett said. "He has a house and a practice there."

"But he has a place here in LA, too, doesn't he?" Jakes asked. "For when he comes to board meetings? I mean, if he's on your board, he comes to meetings, right?"

"Uh, yes."

"So he stays somewhere, right?"

"In a hotel, I assume."

"No," Jakes said. "I bet he has a place. And I bet you have a file on him, a personnel file, with the address in it. And a phone number. I'd like you to get it for me."

"I don't think—"

"Get his file, Mr. Bennett," Jakes said. "I'll bet you have a secretary who can do that for you."

Bennett's smooth face began to shine with perspiration. He picked up his phone and said, "Grace, can you get me Dr. Eugene Reynolds's personnel file please? . . . Yes, bring it in here. Thank you."

"Now tell me about this," Jakes said. He took out a piece of paper folded the long way, unfolded it and handed it to Bennett. I could see it was a photocopy of the memo I'd gotten from Eddie the Stalker. Even the chocolate and ketchup stains had been copied, in color.

Bennett accepted the memo, looked at it. And then, for the first time, something in his face moved.

"Where—where did you get this?"

"It was given to me."

"By whom? This—this is a private memo. No one outside of this building—this company—is supposed to have it."

"Well, I do," Jakes said. "And I'd like you to explain it to me."

"Detective . . ."

"Mr. Bennett?"

Bennett seemed to be running out of air. He loosened his tie.

"Detective . . . this is a private memo . . ."

"I understand that, Mr. Bennett," Jakes said. "What does it mean?"

"Well . . . well . . . I'm not a doctor. I don't really know . . . uh . . . all the details . . ."

"But," Jakes said, pointing, "the memo was signed by you. I assume that means it was drafted by you. Is that correct?"

"Well . . ." Bennett licked his lips. "Well, yes . . ."

Jakes probably saw this all the time, a guilty

person squirming and sweating, but to me it was fascinating. Jakes had told me a long time ago that everyone was guilty of something. This was certainly true of Mr. Carl Bennett.

"So if it was drafted by you and signed by you," Jakes said, "then you can explain to me what it is about, can't you?"

"I—I suppose so."

"Good," Jakes said. "Then I suggest you do it before I have to take you downtown and conduct this conversation in a smaller, less expensively furnished room than this."

Chapter 55

"Detective, our business here is research," Carl Bennett said. "And our focus is an antiaging process that works. This one," he said, tapping the photocopy of the memo, "didn't work. This memo was to keep our people from wasting any more time on it."

"Your people?"

"All the doctors who work on our staff as researchers."

"So this memo went to every doctor on your staff?" Jakes asked.

"That's right."

Jakes took out the business cards he'd collected from the front desk and spread them out on top of Bennett's desk like a winning poker hand. "These doctors?"

"Yes."

"Alex, you got that other card?"

I took out Dr. Reynolds's card, the one Jakes had found in his house in Vegas, and set it on the table with the others, as if it were our ace in the hole.

"And him?" Jakes asked.

Bennett leaned forward to look at the card. "Yes, Dr. Reynolds would have gotten the memo," the administrator said.

"What was wrong with this particular formula?" Jakes asked. He read the name off the memo. "Botchuhylonic acid?"

"It didn't work."

"Be more specific."

"It had . . . specific properties that worked against the antiaging process."

"It made people older instead of younger?" Jakes asked.

"Detective . . . we don't deal in science fiction here," Bennett said. "I'm telling you, it just didn't work."

At that point, a woman entered carrying a folder. She crossed the room and handed it to Bennett. She looked like one of the Whitney Institute's Stepford women, a sister of the smooth-skinned girl downstairs. Her dark hair was up, as were her penciled eyebrows. She was wearing a gray suit and high heels.

"Thank you, Grace," Bennett said, accepting the file from her. "That'll be all."

She left the room without a word, high heels clacking, without looking at Jakes or me. Something was wrong with a woman who didn't look at Detective Frank Jakes. My man is fine.

"This is Dr. Reynolds' personnel file," Bennett said, handing it to Jakes. "Whatever information we have, such as an address, would be in there."

"What else?" It was a slender file.

"His résumé—work history, private information, educational background."

"And both addresses," Jakes said, "in Las Vegas and Los Angeles?"

"Wherever he lived when he joined the Institute."

"And when was that?"

"It's in there."

"You remember, though, don't you?"

Bennett took a deep breath, let it out.

"If I recall correctly, he joined us about five years ago."

"And how long have you been here, Mr. Bennett?"

"Seven years," Bennett said, "when the Institute first started."

"What about Genetic Systems," Jakes asked. "How long have they been around?"

"A very long time," Bennett said. "It's one of the largest drug companies in the country."

"Like Pfizer?" I asked.

Bennett looked at me as if he'd forgotten I was there. I couldn't blame him. Jakes was doing all the talking.

"Perhaps not quite that big," he said.

"I'll take this with me, Mr. Bennett," Jakes said, patting the file, "and return it when we're done."

"You can't—" Bennett started to say, but he changed his mind. "A-all right."

Jakes stood up, tucked the file underneath his

arm. I stood up also, giving Jakes a questioning look. I thought he'd ask more questions of Bennett, who seemed extremely nervous.

"Before we leave, I've got one more question," Jakes said.

Bennett stood.

"What's that?" he asked.

"Was it dangerous? The formula?"

"Dangerous?" Bennett looked confused. "How?"

"I don't know," Jakes said. "Did it . . . hurt people? Maybe make them look older?"

"I'm not the man to answer that, Detective," Bennett said. "My job was only to write the memo and send it out."

"Who gave you the information?"

"The doctor in charge of research on that particular project," Bennett said.

Jakes looked at me, and then at Bennett.

"And who was that, Mr. Bennett?"

Bennett took a deep breath. It didn't surprise us when he said, "Dr. Eugene Reynolds."

Chapter 56

When we got downstairs, Julie watched us walk out the door. Outside we found Jakes's partner, Len Davis, waiting for us.

"You were late," Jakes said.

"I figured you'd start without me." He executed a slight bow in my direction. "Ms. Peterson."

"Hello, Detective Davis," I said. "I'm still Alex to you, you know."

He smiled.

"What do you have there, Frank?" Davis asked.

"Personnel file on Eugene Reynolds."

"Got a home address in there?"

"That's what we're going to find out," Jakes said. "Leave your car here, Len, and come with us."

"Alex is coming, too?" Davis asked.

"That's right."

"Why?"

"Because she gets in trouble when I leave her alone."

"Reminds me of somebody else I know."

* * *

Davis took the wheel of Jakes's car, and I sat in the back. In the passenger's seat, Jakes went through the file folder.

"The Vegas address is in here," he said. "It's only been five years. Most people don't move in that period of time."

"I haven't," I said.

"Me, neither," Jakes said.

"I have," Davis said. "Twice." He looked at me in the rearview mirror and shrugged. "I get bored."

"Okay," Jakes said. "Here's an LA address."

"Nice neighborhood?" Davis asked.

"Brentwood."

"I know the way there," Davis said.

"Let's go," Jakes said.

I touched his shoulder, and he turned to look at me.

"If he was avoiding you in Vegas, what makes you think he'd go to his house here?"

"I don't know," Jakes said. "That's what we're going to find out."

I sat back. What if all this antiaging-formula stuff had nothing to do with Shana's death? Or the girl in Vegas? What if Reynolds was just a doctor trying to get FDA approval on a bad formula?

Well, like Jakes said, that's what we were going to find out.

Davis stopped the car in front of Dr. Reynolds's Brentwood home, an impressive mansion with a long, winding driveway behind a wrought-iron gate that had to be ten feet high.

"How do we get in?" I asked. I almost asked Jakes if he was going to scale this wall the way he had scaled the one in Vegas, but that would have gotten him in trouble with his partner. So I bit my tongue.

"The old-fashioned way," Jakes said, opening his door. "We ring the bell."

He walked to the gate. There was a box next to it with a button and a speaker.

"So how was Vegas?" Davis asked.

"Busy."

"I been meanin' to go to one of those events," he said. "I just never get around to it. Almost made this one, since it was so close, but I was . . . busy."

"Let me know if you want to go to the next one," I said. "I'll get you comped."

"Hey, really?"

"Sure."

Jakes was speaking to someone, bending over so he could talk into the box.

"So, did Frank do anything stupid in Vegas?" Davis asked.

"Stupid?"

He looked at me in the rearview mirror.

"You know what I mean. Bend the law a little bit?"

"Does he do that a lot here?"

"He has his moments."

"Well, I wasn't with him every minute," I said. "Maybe he did."

Jakes came back to the car and opened his door. As he got back in, the gate started to swing inward.

"The lady of the manor will see us."

Davis pulled through the entrance and drove up the driveway. "And the doctor lives in Vegas?" he asked.

"Not sure," Jakes said. He kept to himself the fact that the house in Vegas hadn't looked lived-in at all.

Davis stopped the car behind a new Lexus, and we all got out. We approached the door, and Jakes rang the doorbell. The door was opened by a guy I'd guess to be in his late twenties. He also looked like he spent a substantial amount of time in the gym. He was busting out all over.

"Detective Jakes, we were expecting you. I'm Jones, Toni Jones—with an *i*," he said in a very low voice. "The . . . butler."

"With an *i*?" I asked. "Why an *i*?"

"My psychic told me it was better for my karma."

O-kay, I thought.

"This is my partner, Detective Davis, and Ms. Peterson," Jakes interjected.

The gym rat/butler looked me up and down. I had to give it to him· He had some guns. And muscles in places you'd never imagine.

"Ms. Peterson?" he asked. His voice reminded me of Darth Vader's.

"She's a special adviser working with us," Jakes said.

"Special's right." He looked right at me, and I felt slightly slimed. He was some butler. "This way, please. Pookie is waiting."

Pookie? Was he serious? Apparently so. He led the way, in tight, bun-hugging black pants that were dangerously close to ripping right down the center of his butt crack. I didn't know what to make of this guy. But I didn't have time to think about it. I was about to meet Pookie.

Chapter 57

The house was simply spectacular. I didn't know whether Pookie had an interior decorator or what, but someone had great, and very expensive, taste. As opposed to the Vegas pad, this place was definitely lived-in. As I looked around the beautifully appointed living room, I noticed the grand piano was adorned with a plethora of photographs. Interesting, I thought to myself. Photos of Dr. Reynolds were conspicuously missing.

Jones led us through the living room and another gorgeous room I assumed to be the library, to the back of the house. We walked through the doors and found ourselves in an atrium complete with glass walls and ceiling. Lush green trees were swaying in the breeze, and through the windows I could see a rolling lawn opening first to a pool surrounded by white statues and then, ultimately, a panoramic view of the Santa Monica foothills. As if this weren't enough to take in, we were greeted by a woman lying on the floor with her legs in the air, her feet tucked behind her ears, like a contortionist. She looked as if her head were attached to her, um . . . This should be a fascinating conversation. I found myself wondering how long she could hold that pose.

"Pooks, Detectives Davis and Jakes," Jones said. "Oh, and Ms. Peterson." He looked at me, and again I felt slimed.

"Thank you, Toni."

Pookie disengaged her feet from behind her ears and assumed a seated position on the floor. Then she suddenly jumped to both feet and stood directly in front of us. She was wearing very snug yoga tights and a cropped top. She was hot. A mane of auburn hair framed a heart-shaped face and wide green eyes. Her body was voluptuous, but at the same time extremely toned. She reminded me of Tina Louise—you know, Ginger from Gilligan's Island. Pooks was a good forty years old and she was gorgeous, exuding an innate sexuality. Toni's job description was becoming a little clearer by the minute.

"Will you bring us some drinks, please?"

"What would you like?" he asked.

"Surprise us."

"You got it," he said, and left.

"Mrs. Reynolds, my name is Detective—"

"I'm Ms. Wisniewski now. Janet Wisniewski, but I like to be called Pookie." She smiled conspiratorially. "It pisses off Gene." She looked at me and then suddenly said, "Omigod. You're Alexis Peterson, from *The Yearning Tide*!"

"*The Bare and the Brazen* now," Davis corrected.

"That's right!" she said, pointing at Davis. "Holy cow! It is you, isn't it?"

"It's me," I said.

"Wow," she said again. Then, "It's so nice to meet you."

"Nice to meet you, too, Mrs.—Pookie."

"Detective Jakes, Detective Davis. What can I do for all of you?"

"Actually," Jakes said, "we were looking for your husband."

"Ex-husband. Soon to be, anyway. Why do you want Gene? What's he done?"

"What makes you think he's done anything, Pookie?" Jakes said.

"Well, you are the police, right? So I'm assuming the son of a bitch is in trouble. Is he?"

"You and your husband don't get along?"

"We're not getting a divorce because we adore each other, Detective," she deadpanned.

"We'd like to ask him some questions concerning a homicide," Jakes said.

"Gene really stepped in it this time, huh?"

"How long have you been married?"

"Ten years," she said. "We met in Vegas. I was a showgirl, front row center. That's when I got the nickname Pookie. Gene called me that. He was an up-and-coming doctor. And we fell in love."

"So what happened?"

"He wasn't the man I thought he was," she said. "And as he got bigger and more successful, I started to be an embarrassment on his arm. He stopped calling me Pookie, and wanted everyone else to, as well. Not respectable, and all that bullshit. Excuse my French."

"He didn't like the idea of your having been a showgirl?" Davis asked.

"Apparently. It's not something I'm ashamed of, though."

"So he doesn't live here?" Jakes said.

"Hasn't for years."

"What do you know about his work with the Whitney Institute and Genetic Systems?" Jakes asked.

"Nothing," she said. "But I sure as hell wouldn't let him work on me."

"You don't think he's a good doctor?"

"He's gotten into the research side over the past few years," she said. "That office he has in Vegas? It's run by partners. He only does a few surgeries, mostly breast augmentations. I guess he likes the female clientele."

"So you don't know about his research?"

"I told you. Nothing. I don't know anything, and I don't want to."

"I see," Jakes said. "Well, if you see him or talk to him—"

"I won't," she assured us. "Not a chance. Sorry. I guess you'll have to keep looking for him."

The three of us exchanged glances. Was she telling the truth, or protecting her husband? Was this an act?

Toni Jones walked in pushing a drink cart. It looked like he had decided to surprise us with martinis.

"What will everyone have?" she asked, smiling.

"We're on the clock, Pookie," Jakes said.

Chapter 58

As Davis drove us away from Pookie's house, he complained that he'd missed lunch.

"You're right." I said, looking at my watch. "It's after four—almost time for dinner."

"I'm starving."

At that point, Jakes's cell phone rang. He held a finger up to us and answered.

"What do you say the three of us get some dinner?" Davis asked.

"I already have plans, but I thought you didn't like me anymore, Len."

"Ms. Peterson, why would you say something like that?"

"Well, you used to call me Alex, but ever since I left *The Yearning Tide*, you've been calling me Ms. Peterson."

"Oh, well," Davis stammered, "I was just, uh, disappointed. You know, as a fan of the show, and of Tiffany's—I mean, yours . . ."

My phone beeped, rescuing Len from having to

stammer out the rest of his apology. It was a text from George.

Dun erly. Where r u?

B there n 15, I texted back.

Jakes and I ended our calls at exactly the same time.

"That was Cushing," he said.

"Cushing?" I asked.

"She said one of the girls who lived with Linda Bronsky is dead."

"What?"

"Which one?" Davis asked.

"Susan Couture," he answered. Then he looked at me. "The girl we spoke to together."

"My God," I said. "That poor girl. How?"

"Same way as Shana and Linda."

"What about the other girl? Elizabeth?" I asked.

"Cushing says she was a witness and is on the run."

"Does Cushing think she's coming here?" Davis asked.

"Why would she think that?" I asked.

"She does. She said Elizabeth has family here," Jakes said. And then to me, "We have to check this out. Without you. Sorry."

"No problem. I have plans with George, anyway. Remember? We're close to the studio. Just drop me off at my car."

"Sure," Jakes said.

"Call me as soon as you know something, okay?" I still wanted to be kept in the loop.

Jakes pulled into the artist's entrance, and I poked my head out of the car so the guard could see it was me.

"Hi, Ms. Peterson!" He opened the gate for us as we drove through. The car stopped and I jumped out. I bent down to give Jakes a kiss, but we both hesitated with Davis there. Awkward.

"Like I don't know you two are involved. Kiss her already!" Len shouted as he turned the other way to give us privacy. We kissed. Quickly.

I was walking down the hallway toward the elevator when George came barreling around the corner, almost colliding with me.

"Oh, sorry, honey! I thought we were meeting out front," George said.

"I thought we'd just walk out through the back of the studio and go to the Grove for dinner."

The Grove is a very trendy mall that caters to the rich and famous. A TMZ favorite, it's also, conveniently, in our studio's backyard.

"I don't care where we go as long as they serve food and drink. Onward!" And we linked arms and headed for the rear of the studio.

On the way over to the Grove, I told him about our day: talking to Mr. Bennett at the Institute, and later on to the soon-to-be-ex–Mrs. Reynolds, Pookie.

"Ooh," he said, when I was done. "Tell me again about the man with the long black ponytail. Toni with an *i*."

"Never mind; you're married," I said. "Besides, he's not your type. If he's gay, he'd be rough trade."

"Oh, well," George said. "At my age, my rough-trade days are over. What about Pookie?"

"Who cares about Pookie? I mean, she's gorgeous, in a Tina Louise kind of way. And very, very limber." George looked his question. "You don't want to know."

We were heading out the security gates that led to the Grove's back entrance when Mickey, a security guard, stopped us.

"Hey, Ms. Peterson? Did that guy find you?"

"What guy, Mickey?"

"He didn't say his name. I assumed he was a fan, but he said he knew you. He was wondering if you were here today."

"Huh. No. Nobody found me. You're probably right about his being a fan. Thanks."

We pushed through the gates as Mickey called to me, "You have all sorts of fans, don't you?"

"All kinds of fans, Mickey. All kinds!"

George pulled me ahead. "C'mon, already. I'm starving!"

Daylight saving time had "fallen back," so even though it was only five o'clock, it was already dark outside. George and I were catching up on our gossip as we walked in the alley behind the Grove. We were taking a shortcut to our favorite restaurant, Maggiano's. Out of the corner of my eye, I noticed someone walking across from and a little behind us by the parking structure. I glanced over and was taken aback. At first I didn't think I was right, but I was. He was hard to miss.

What, I thought, is Toni Jones doing at the Grove?

Chapter 59

"What's wrong?" George asked when he saw the look on my face.

"Look there," I said, "by the parking structure."

We both looked, and nobody was there.

"I don't see anything," George said.

"He was there."

"Who?"

I turned to look at George. "Toni Jones."

"Rough Trade?" George asked.

"In the flesh."

George looked again.

"A coincidence?" he asked.

"I don't know. Wait! That's who Mickey was referring to! Toni must have been looking for me at the studio. He must have followed us here."

"Maybe he wants to talk to you."

"So pick up the phone. And why did he leave so abruptly just now?" The more I thought about it, the stranger it seemed. "I don't have a good feeling about this. Why is he here? What does he want from me? Did Pookie send him?"

"But why?" George asked. "Are you sure it isn't a coincidence? Everyone comes to the Grove, you know."

"They don't usually hang out in the alley, George. And it had to be him at the studio, too."

George thought about that for a second.

"Well, how about if I walk around and have a look?" he asked.

"By yourself?"

"Please," he said, drawing himself up. "For you, I can be the man."

I actually considered it for a moment.

"No, no," I said, waving his offer away. "Why start now? Ha! Just kidding. This is silly. Let's just walk around the corner and see if he's there and what he's up to—together."

"Okay," he said, "but remember my offer."

I rubbed his arm and said, "I'll always remember your sweet offer to be the man, Georgie."

He put his arm out for me to take and we walked back toward the studio.

"Uh-oh," George said, when we were three steps around the corner. "Is that him, right over there?"

Toni was lounging against the wall of the parking structure, under a streetlight. He was wearing a muscle shirt that showed off his biceps and huge shoulders.

"That's him." I looked at his eyes. "He looks pissed off. I mean, really pissed off."

"Honey," he said, "that's the Incredible Hulk."

"He's big all right—"

"Alex, see the tattoo on his arm? The eye?"

I did see it. I looked at George inquisitively. Then it dawned on me. The Incredible Hulk at the Halloween party had the same tattoo. An eye. Toni. With an eye!

"Holy crap," I said. "He was at Hef's."

Just then, Toni started walking toward us. The light from the streetlamp reflected off something shiny in his right hand. I was sure it was a knife! I grabbed George's arm in one hand and my cell in another.

"Walk!" I said to George. "Now!"

I hit speed dial and, luckily, Jakes picked up.

"Jakes, thank God!"

"Alex, what is it?"

"He's here."

"Who's where?"

"Toni Jones. George and I are in the alley behind the Grove. And he just appeared. And he was at the studio earlier, looking for me."

"Okay, relax," he said. "Maybe he just wants to talk to you."

"Jakes! He was at the Halloween party, too." I said. "And I'm pretty sure he has a knife."

It didn't even take a second for it to sink in.

"Are you around people?"

"No! We're in an alleyway." I ran to a door behind a boutique and pulled. Locked! I turned around; Toni was still fifty yards away, but slowly gaining on us. "He's getting closer!"

"Find a crowd. You have to find people!"

"We have to get inside the Grove, George! Where is the opening?" George was as white as a sheet. He stared at me with eyes as big as saucers.

"Up ahead. A few yards ahead. We'll be at the fountain." I looked at him, then realized he was right.

"The fountain. The dancing waters. That's where we're going!"

"I can be there in fifteen. I'm not sure what he's up to, but let's not take any chances. I'll call for backup and they'll be there soon. Go! Don't hang up, Alex. Just go!" And we started walking faster, checking every door to the stores as we ran. Each one was locked.

"Oh, shit!" George exclaimed. I turned and saw that Toni was gaining. He looked all pumped up, like he was going to explode.

"He's 'roided," George whimpered.

Chapter 60

"I've seen it a lot in West Hollywood with the body-builders. They're pumped up on steroids and have a certain insane look when they've overdone it. They're crazy nuts, Alex! Violent! Call the cops!"

His voice had risen to a squeal. I guess this was him being the man. He grabbed my arm tighter.

"Ow! I'm still on with Jakes. Jakes, are you still there?" Nothing. "Jakes! Shit! We got cut off. George, just stay calm!" He gave me a withering look and glanced behind us.

"Run!" I looked behind us and saw that Toni had started to run toward us. He must have noticed we were close to a break in the stores and were heading into the main Grove walkway. We started sprinting. We reached the corner only to collide into a security guard.

"Thank God! Sorry, officer. Guard. Whatever!" George cried.

"What are you doing? You almost knocked me over!" The guard was a young man, but wore the annoyed expression that most mall security guards acquire after time on the job. He ignored George and looked at me.

"What's the problem, ma'am?"

"There's a man chasing us," I said, out of breath.

"Take it easy. Where is he?"

"Right there . . ." I turned to show him, but Toni was gone.

"He was there, I swear. He followed us and he's dangerous."

"What did he do to you?"

"Well, nothing . . . yet."

"What did he say?"

"Nothing."

"Ma'am, how do you know he means you any harm?"

"Look," I said, "I'm pretty sure he had a knife. See, I'm working with the police on a murder case." Well, I was. And we needed him to act.

Now he scowled at me.

"You're a cop?" he asked. "Let's see some ID."

"No, I'm not a cop," I said, "but I'm working with the police."

He stepped back.

"I know who you are. You're on that show—*Too Late for Yesterday*, right?"

"Yeah, right," I said. Wrong show, but it didn't matter.

"Look, look, there he is!" George said, grabbing the security guard's arm.

I turned and saw Toni coming toward us.

"You've got to stop him," I said. "The police are on the way."

"I'll talk to him," he said.

"Take out your gun," George said.

"I can't do that, sir," he said. "There are rules I have to follow. Just relax and I'll talk to him."

"Officer—" George started, but he was already headed to intercept Toni.

"Okay," George said. "It's gonna be okay."

We walked a few feet away and watched as the guard stopped Toni and spoke to him. Toni jabbed a forefinger into the guard's chest. The guard slapped it away, but then Toni got even closer. The guard put his hand on his gun, but when I saw the flash of light on the knife, I knew he was too late.

"No!" I said. I thought I screamed it, but it came out a whisper.

Toni stepped in close to the guard, and the guard's body jerked.

"Oh, my God," I said, "he stabbed him!"

"Oh no . . ." George breathed.

Toni looked at both of us over the guard's shoulder and grinned. He slowly lowered the guard to the ground, and pulled him around the corner into the alleyway.

"George, we have to go."

"B-but, the guard—"

"He wants to kill me. Us, since you're with me. Let's go. Now!"

"The fountain." George snapped to. "Let's go!"

Chapter 61

As we were running toward the center of the Grove, I dialed Jakes. No service! Where were the cops? I turned around and saw Toni behind us, waiting for a trolley car to pass. We were almost at the fountain. It was similar to the dancing waters in front of the Bellagio in Vegas, only on a much smaller scale. Still, it attracted people for the show it supplied every half hour. They gathered around, forming a human wall, which was exactly what we needed at that moment.

"That dude is crazy! Where's Jakes?" George asked. I was wondering the same thing as he pressed up against me from behind.

The music started and the waters began to dance. People oohed and aahed as they watched. George and I kept looking around to see whether Toni had somehow moved in on us through the crowd. I kept expecting to feel the blade of a knife cutting into me from behind.

It occurred to me that Jakes's idea for us to go someplace crowded probably would have worked if Toni had been armed with a gun, but a knife in a crowd? With all of us pressed so tightly against each other . . .

"There must be more security around," George said.

"Georgie," I said, in his ear, "we should split up."

"Why?"

"Because he's after me," I said. "He'd let you go."

He looked at me, shocked. "I wouldn't leave you!" he said. "My God, Alex—"

"I don't want you to get hurt, George."

"Well, I don't want you to die!" he shot back.

"Maybe he doesn't want to kill me," I said. "Maybe he just wants to take me somewhere."

"Yes," he said, "to kill you. No, no, we're staying together." He grabbed my hand and held it tightly. "If he wants to hurt you, he'll have to go through me."

I squeezed his hand and kissed his cheek. Abruptly, Toni Jones appeared behind George. Georgie jumped, as if he'd just received an electric shock, but the look on his face was one of pain.

Toni grinned at me and showed me his knife over George's shoulder, with blood on the tip. Casually, he wiped it on the sleeve of George's shirt.

Oh, God, I thought. He stabbed George!

My best friend sagged. I felt an overwhelming desire to jump on Toni and gouge his eyes out. Toni must have sensed it.

"I just stuck it in a half inch, Alex," Toni hissed. "Just enough to hurt, but not enough to kill him."

He looked around as people walked away.

"Let's just stay nice and close to each other so folks can't tell what's goin' on," he said. "We're gonna walk out of here nice and slow, like three really good friends." He slapped George on the back, making him jump again. I could see underneath Toni's shirt. Lots of bumps and grooves. Muscles, I guessed, but on some crazy, overblown scale.

Steroids, all right. And lots of them.

George still looked pained and scared, but smiled.

"Good," Toni said. "That's good. Come on, now. Let's go toward the Farmers Market. We'll go out that way. And I *will* kill your chubby little friend. So don't try anything."

Well, I thought, my heart thumping in my chest, that's dumb. We were being led away, probably to be killed. Why would we not try something?

Chapter 62

Toni stayed behind George and me, using the knife to push each of us ahead of him. I tried to jerk away, and he wrapped one arm around my waist and pulled me tightly to him.

"Be nice," he hissed in my ear.

"Why should I?" I asked. "You're going to kill me, right? Why shouldn't I just start screaming?"

"Because I'll push this knife into your chubby friend so far, you'll see the tip of it on the other side."

"Could you please stop with the *chubby*? He's very sensitive about his weight." George looked at me quickly with a *Now?* look.

I was scared, but didn't want to show it.

"Why'd you cut Shana's throat?" I asked. "She didn't have to die that way, did she?"

"Who said I killed Shana?"

"If not you, then Pookie. Right?"

"Shut up and stop trying to distract me."

I got an extra hard shove.

"And Linda? The girl in Vegas? And what about Susan?" I asked.

"I don't remember their names," Toni said. "I just do the job."

"So you're for hire?"

He laughed. "I'm not a pro, if that's what you mean," he said, "but I'm earnin' my money, believe me."

I dug in my heels. We were walking around the fountain, so there was still water on our right.

"No," I said. "Let George go. I'll go with you, but let him go."

"Sorry," Toni said. "Can't do that. He's seen me, you idiot."

Then George shocked us all.

"Run, Alex!" he shouted. Then he turned, spread his arms and took Toni into the fountain with him. The look on Toni's face showed how shocked he was.

I was shocked, too—too shocked to run. I wanted to grab George and help him out of the fountain before Toni could climb out, but at that moment, somebody grabbed me from behind.

I started to fight.

"Easy, Alex," Jakes said in my ear. "We're here now."

Suddenly, there were a lot of blue uniforms climbing into the fountain, grabbing George and Toni, hauling both of them out.

"Finally!" George said, looking at Jakes with exasperation. "What the heck took you so long?"

"Not him," Jakes said, putting his hand on George's shoulder. "He's with me."

The policeman holding on to George nodded and let him go.

"Georgie, you're my hero!" I cried, throwing my arms around him.

"Ow!" George said.

"Oh," I said, letting him go. "Jakes, George got stabbed in the back. Are you all right, Georgie?"

"I banged my knee when we fell into the water," George said. Jakes turned him around and looked at his lower back.

"Just about a pinprick," he said. "But we'll have the EMTs look at it."

"Did you find that poor security guard?" I asked, as Len Davis walked George over to the ambulance.

"Someone found him," Jakes said. "He's gonna be okay."

"Toni said he wasn't a pro," I said.

"That much was obvious."

"I think he killed Shana and those girls in Vegas," I said.

"Well, we'll confirm that soon enough," Jakes told me. Cushing found Elizabeth Sessions, and she's bringing her here to LA. She'll take a look at Toni Jones and identify him."

"Then it's over," I said.

"No," Jakes said. "We need the person he was working for."

"We know who it is," I said.

The police had cordoned off the fountain so that no one else was standing near it. People were watching the action from a distance. I heard the handcuffs being snapped on to Toni.

"He works for Pookie."

"We know he works for her," Jakes said, "but we don't know that he killed for her. We'll hold him for attempted murder of the guard, and threatening you and George. Maybe he'll give Pookie up."

We looked over at Toni, who was grinning at both of us.

"There's only one problem," Jakes said.

"What's that?"

He looked at me and said, "I think he's crazy."

Chapter 63

"Where are we going now?"

Jakes and I were in his car. George had been taken to the hospital. Toni had been booked on multiple charges, including the attempted murder of the security guard. Davis was taking care of the paperwork.

"Pookie's house," Jakes said. "If she sent Toni after you, she's probably waiting to hear from him. Well, that's not gonna happen. She'll be hearing from us."

"Are you going to arrest her?"

"I can't," Jakes said. "Not unless she confesses, or I get a call from Len saying that Toni gave her up. But I can take her in for questioning."

"What if she's not involved at all?"

"We'll find that out, too."

"And why am I along?" I asked.

"If she's expecting you to be killed tonight, I want to see the look on her face when you walk into her house, alive and kicking."

"I get to kick her?" I asked hopefully.

He smiled, took his eyes off the road just for a moment to look at me, and said, "We'll see."

When we reached the house, we found the front gates wide open. As we drove up the drive, we saw why. We had to park behind two other cars—a Lexus and a BMW, both brand-new.

"Looks like she's got company," I said.

"I've got an idea," he said as he put the car in reverse and backed it down the driveway, out of sight. "They won't hear the car doors from here."

"What are we going to do?" I asked.

"We're going to see just who's visiting Pookie," he said. "We might get lucky."

"You think the doctor might be in there?"

"I'm not sure Miss Pookie is smart enough to have planned all this," Jakes said as we got out. "Whatever *all this* turns out to be."

"Because she's a woman?" I asked. "You think a man has to be behind it? Like Reynolds? Or Bennett?"

"Don't get your I Am Woman shorts in a bunch," he said. "It's not because she's a woman. I just didn't get the impression she was that smart. And before you say it, it's not because she was a showgirl."

"Just clarifying. Maniacal killers aren't gender specific, you know. They come in all shapes and sizes. And sexes. Don't you watch A&E?"

He looked at me and shook his head.

"I've been thinking all along that this whole antiaging deal means a lot of money to everybody involved," Jakes said. "The doctor, Bennett and Pookie."

"So you think they're behind it together?"

"It's all about getting FDA approval," Jakes said, "for a product that doesn't work. And who could blow the whistle on them?"

"Anybody who tried the product," I said.

"Right," Jakes said. "The showgirls in Vegas and Shana."

"But wait. Why would Bennett send out a memo saying the product didn't work?"

We were working our way up the driveway, back toward the house, talking in whispers.

"I don't know," Jakes said. "Maybe he got involved after the memo was sent. Reynolds could've offered him a ton of money to keep quiet."

"They could have tried to get all the copies of the memo back, but they couldn't get the one that Stalker Eddie grabbed."

"And he gave it to you."

"But where'd he get it?"

"My first bet would be her garbage can. Ketchup and chocolate, remember? He's a stalker," Jakes said. "Those are all loose ends we'll have to tie up, but for now, let's see what's going on inside that house."

Chapter 64

We saw lights blasting into the sky from the back of the house. They must have been in the atrium.

We had to circle around the house, but as we got back there, we could hear the sound of raised voices.

Luckily, there was a lot of foliage in the back. We were able to stay out of sight while getting close enough to hear what was said.

Neither of us had ever seen Dr. Reynolds in person, only in photos, but we recognized him. He was in the atrium along with Carl Bennett and Janet "Pookie" Wisniewski.

". . . crazy," Reynolds was saying. "You've always been a crazy bitch, but this takes the cake."

Reynolds was visibly agitated as he stood in the center of the room, wearing an impeccably tailored suit that seemed to be itchy. He couldn't keep still as he berated his wife.

Standing off to one side was Carl Bennett. His suit was no less expensive, but he didn't have the shoulders to fill it out as well. He had an alarmed expression on his face as he watched the happy couple.

Pookie was dressed for a leisurely night at home in tight-fitting yoga pants and a body-hugging hoodie. She was standing hipshot, with a martini glass in one hand, the other on her hip. If I had been a man, I would have thought, What a body. Oh, who am I kidding? I thought it anyway.

"If you were the doctor you think you are," she said to her husband calmly, "we wouldn't be in this mess."

"If you weren't a crazy, sex-starved bitch—" he said, but she cut him off.

"Sex starved? I wonder if that has anything to do with being married to you!"

Reynolds looked at his watch.

"Where is this muscle-bound boyfriend of yours?" he demanded.

"I don't know—I told you! He's out of control." Pookie said. "He said he was going to kill Alexis for me. The idiot! I tried to stop him. I did!"

I got a chill down my spine. It was eerie hearing someone talk about murdering someone. Specifically me. I jumped a bit when Jakes touched my arm.

"Okay. Get back to the car."

"What? I thought you wanted to see the look on her face when she saw me?"

"Don't need to now. I need you in the car."

"Where are you going?"

"I want to see if I can find a way in," he said.

"Why don't you wait for backup?"

"They're on the way," he said. "And Len will meet us here if he gets anything from Toni. So do what I tell you and—"

"—Get back in the car. Yes, sir."

He waited until he saw me heading back and then melted away into the darkness. Jakes must have figured he'd already heard enough to incriminate them. I figured he was trying to get inside to make an arrest. I hesitated and then gingerly walked back to the atrium, knowing he'd be pissed. But I just had to see what was going to happen next.

I got there in time to see Carl Bennett suddenly move closer to the battling couple. They dropped their voices. I decided to try to move closer so I could hear better. Bad move. The ground beneath my feet was soft, squishy. In one spot, it was too soft. It felt as if the ground was giving way, so I took a quick step to try to keep my balance. Apparently, a gardener hadn't put away all his tools, and I stepped on a rake. The handle came up and hit me in the face. I let out an inadvertent yelp and tumbled over backward, stunned. How very Three Stooges!

I sat up, my hand pressed to my forehead where the wooden handle had hit me. When I looked up, there were two people looking down at me: Dr. Eugene Reynolds and Carl Bennett.

"Who's this?" Reynolds asked.

"That," Bennett said, "is Alexis Peterson."

"Oh?" Reynolds tilted his head as if he were examining something under a microscope.

"I think we should help the lady up and bring her inside," he said.

Chapter 65

Pookie handed me a martini. Under the circumstances, I took it. The circumstances being that my head hurt and I was among people who were probably trying to figure out a way to kill me.

"Thank you," I said.

I was sitting in a chair, and the three of them were standing in front of me. I wondered where Jakes was.

"That's quite a welt on your forehead," Pookie said. "I hope you're not considering suing me. But then, you were trespassing on my property."

"I rang the bell. Nobody answered. I came around to see whether anyone was home."

Pookie smiled. "That's a quick lie. You're good. Would you like my husband to have a look at you? See if you have a concussion? He's not much of a doctor anymore, but I think he can still do that much."

"Janet!" Reynolds said.

"Pookie!" she spit back. Only spite could have

been the reason she was so attached to *that* nick-name.

This was the first close look I'd had at the good doctor. He was handsome, in an effete sort of way—smooth, pale skin; gentle blues eyes; long-fingered, graceful hands . . . the hands of a surgeon? Or a murderer?

"What are we going to do with her?" Bennett asked. "She must have been outside listening—"

"Shut up, Carl!" Pookie snapped.

"We all know she heard us. She was standing right outside," Carl hissed at her.

I looked at Pookie. "You sent your boyfriend to kill me, you bitch!" I was stalling for time. And Jakes.

Pookie looked truly upset. She looked to her husband. "I didn't. I swear. I swear!"

"He tried to kill a security guard."

"Why, Janet?" Gene looked at Pookie. "Why did you bring somebody else in on this?"

"No! I'm telling you, Toni has gone crazy. He's lost all control. How stupid do you think I am? Alexis is with the cops!"

"How stupid do I think you are? Stupid enough to get us into this mess!" Gene snapped back.

"*You* got us into this mess. By being such a chick-enshit. When it became clear your precious formula wasn't going to be approved, you were ready to give up. I saved it by stalling for time!"

"Janet, listen—" Bennett started.

"And you!" she said, pointing a finger at him. "You had to write that damn memo. If it wasn't for me, copies would have gone out. I'm the one who saved the whole deal. All we had to do was get rid of a few witnesses."

I wondered whether she knew that at least one memo had slipped through. If Eddie the Stalker had gotten it from Shana's house, how did Shana get it?

"Janet, you can't—" Reynolds started, but she cut him off with a stare. It was clear those two men were dominated by this woman.

"You." She spit the word. "Feeling sorry for 'poor Shana.' Her face hurt and she needed drugs. Give her a prescription! You didn't need to have her over to your place. Stupidly leaving the memo out where she could see it. That's why she had to be killed. Because of you! She would have gone to the FDA. And we'd have nothing to show for all our work!"

So that's how Shana got her hands on the memo! And she probably tossed it in her garbage, where Stalker Eddie found it.

"If you'd had the nerve to kill her when I told you to, we wouldn't be in this mess." Pookie went on. "I wouldn't have had to dress like a wood nymph and do it myself."

Then I realized what she'd just said. So she was the girl who had called Shana away to the phony photo shoot.

"We shouldn't be talking about this in front of her," Bennett said.

"What difference does it make, you moron? We have to eliminate her and then get out of here. Now."

"I think you're just a little too late, Pookie."

That voice made me sigh with relief. Jakes was standing at the doorway, holding a gun.

"How did you get into my house?" Pookie demanded.

"I found an open window. You should be more careful."

"You can't just break into someone's house!"

"So sue me," Jakes said. "After I've arrested all of you for murder, and conspiracy to commit murder." He looked at me and asked, "Are you all right?"

"Fine, now," I said, and finished my martini.

Bennett started to cry. It was pathetic. Reynolds just looked like a beaten man.

Pookie, on the other hand, assumed a haughty attitude. She stuck out her boobs and stuck up her nose.

"You can't prove a thing," she said. "My lawyer will have me out in an hour."

"What about those two?" Jakes asked.

"Let them get their own lawyer," she said.

"And the muscle boy downtown? He's talking up a storm."

"He's got so many steroids in his system, he doesn't know what he's saying or doing," Pookie said.

"Well, we'll sort it all out downtown," Jakes said. "Let's go, folks. Alex, come over here."

Before getting up, I put the empty martini glass down on the drink cart. That was the only reason I saw Pookie pick up a small-caliber gun from the bookshelf behind the cart.

"Jakes! Gun!" I shouted.

I leaped for Pookie, hoping to throw off her aim as she raised the gun with her right hand. She swung her left arm at me and knocked me into the drink cart. The cart and I tumbled to the floor. She wasn't just limber; she was strong!

But I'd cost her some time, and before she could pull the trigger, Jakes pulled his. I was on my back in a martini puddle, so I heard, rather than saw, the bullet hit her. I also heard her cry out. Her gun fell from her hand and she slumped to the floor.

"Janet!" Reynolds said, rushing to her.

Jakes rushed forward, too, and snatched her gun from the floor.

"It's Pookie, you asshole," she said before passing out.

Bennett took the opportunity to run from the room.

"He's getting away," I said, pointing.

"Not a chance," Jakes said, putting out his hand and pulling me to my feet. "There are cops outside, all around the house."

I let him hug me to him with his left arm as he continued to point his gun at the couple with his right.

"You shot her!" Reynolds said accusingly.

"You bet I did," Jakes said. "You're a doctor. Take

care of her. I'll need her on her feet to walk into a cell."

I looked down at Pookie, who was out cold. Blood spread from her shoulder, down her chest and arm.

"She killed Shana herself," I said. "She dressed up as a wood nymph. George'll be able to identify her."

"Maybe she did the showgirls herself, too," Jakes said. "When Cushing gets here with Elizabeth Sessions, maybe she'll ID her."

"What about Toni?"

"Just muscle, I guess. She's right about one thing, though. He's loaded up on steroids. He doesn't even remember stabbing the guard."

"I'm just glad it's over," I said. "It is over, isn't it?"

"Should be. You took a big chance, jumping for that gun," Jakes said.

"Yeah, she swatted me away like a fly. She is freakishly strong!"

"But you kept her from shooting me," he said. "You're my hero."

"Well, that's nice to hear for a change. I guess heroes aren't gender specific, either." I smiled, leaning against him.

"By the way," he asked, "how'd you get that lump on your forehead?"

Chapter 66

It was late the next evening, and we were lying together on a chaise in back of my house. We snuggled under a big, comfy blanket thrown over us against the winter chill. Mom and Sarah were asleep. Jakes had spent the entire day tying up loose ends, and now he was filling me in.

"Elizabeth Sessions identified Pookie as the woman who killed Susan Couture. She tried to kill Sessions, but she got away." He took a sip of red wine.

"What about Linda Bronson?"

"We don't know. Pookie isn't talking."

"What about Toni?"

"He's talking," Jakes said. "He's got a classic case of 'roid rage. In his own demented way, he wanted to prove his love to her, so he took it upon himself to go that extra mile."

"By killing me?"

Jakes nodded. "George identified Toni as the man who was dressed as the Incredible Hulk at Hef's party. Then he identified Pookie as the wood nymph, the one who lured Shana away to a phony photo shoot."

"So Pookie killed Shana?"

"That's what Toni says."

"Are you sure he's not just trying to cover his own ass?" I asked.

"We considered that maybe he killed them all for her, and now just doesn't want to take the fall alone. It's a possibility, but I don't think it's the case."

"So what do you think?"

"You saw her. She had all of those men wrapped around her little finger."

"She's a tough broad, all right."

"We questioned Dr. Reynolds and Bennett. They back up what Pookie said, that it was all her idea to kill the women who had tried the antiaging cream."

"How did they get their hands on it, anyway?"

"The three girls in Vegas had boob jobs by Dr. Reynolds, and he gave them a free trial of the cream."

"And Shana?" I asked, trying to take it all in.

"Same thing. Reynolds did her breast augmentation, and convinced her to try the cream. She was the one who threatened to go to the FDA. She saw that the formula worked and caused regeneration of cells. Then, after a period of time, it began to reverse itself and actually made the cells degenerate. Ultimately, it caused these women to look even older than they did before they used it."

"It made their skin look younger, and then reversed itself? That's brutal."

"When we asked them to look more closely, both

MEs—LA and Vegas—found the skin around Linda Bronson and Shana's eyes had somehow aged—gotten thinner and more susceptible to wrinkles. They also had traces of the same drugs in their systems."

"That botch— botchu—"

"Botchuhylonic acid, yes. And the painkillers. As the formula started to degenerate, apparently it also caused these women a significant amount of pain."

"Why didn't the three showgirls go to the FDA?"

"Reynolds convinced them he was going to fix the problem."

"And what? He realized he couldn't?"

"He realized he couldn't in time to get FDA approval. So Pookie took it upon herself to 'fix' the problem."

"Why not Reynolds? Or Bennett? Why did she take it upon herself? That seems kind of extreme."

Jakes ran his hand over his face. He looked so tired. I rubbed the back of his neck, stroked his hair.

"They all had something to gain, but Reynolds says Pookie wanted to make sure it was approved before their divorce was final. FDA approval meant more money for her. Lots more."

"What were they going to do once the cream was approved?" I asked.

"Bennett said they had major cosmetics companies champing at the bit to get a hold of this cream, if it was approved. Once it was, Reynolds would fix the problem before he sold it."

"He still thought he could fix it?" I said.

"If not, by the time the FDA realized the product was

dangerous, Reynolds and Bennett would have already made millions. They would have left the country."

"Can you arrest her without a confession?"

"We've got George's ID putting her at Hef's party and we've got Sessions, who saw her slit Couture's throat in Vegas. We can charge her, no doubt about it."

"And the men?"

"Federal raps on the whole FDA thing, conspiracy to commit murder, attempted-murder rap for Toni on the security guard."

We sat in silence for a while, sipping our wine.

"So, it's all over?"

"Far from over for me," Jakes said, "but for you, yes."

"I can't help but feel sad for Shana. For all those women. All because of a few wrinkles? It's so pointless." I shook my head. "I think I'll start a women's movement. The more wrinkles you have—and I'll throw cellulite in there, too—the more beautiful our society considers you!"

"Now, *that* would be dangerous. You'd put a lot of people out of business." He kissed me and finished his wine. "I'd better get going."

I walked him through the house. We put the glasses down on the coffee table, and went the rest of the way holding hands.

"Hey," I said, "how did Eddie the Stalker get hold of that memo?"

"We're gonna find him and ask. Like I said before, my guess is he got it from Shana's trash."

When we got to the door, he pulled me to him and held me tight.

"We have to talk," he said. He was giving me those dreamy eyes and the husky voice that made me want to do stuff other than talk.

"About . . . ?" I moved in closer to him.

"I'm starting to think the only way to keep you out of danger is to be near you more. A lot more." Was he saying what I thought he was saying? "When this is all wrapped up, maybe it's time we talked about a real commitment." I think my face froze along with my voice. I looked from his eyes to his mouth, back to his eyes.

"Okay."

He kissed me tenderly, and then he walked out the door. I stood there watching in a mild state of shock until he drove away. I locked the door and numbly walked into the kitchen. Commitment? As in *M* words? *Moving in together* or *marriage*? It dawned on me that it didn't sound so scary anymore. It sounded good and made me feel warm inside and, dare I say, happy. I looked around at my little house. Where could we possibly fit all of his stuff? That's when I saw the envelope on the kitchen counter.

It was a business-sized white envelope. The return address was one I didn't recognize: EDDLESTEIN AND BALLARD, ATTORNEYS AT LAW. This couldn't be good. My hands started to shake as I opened it.

It was from a lawyer representing Randy. He was suing me for custody of Sarah.